Jump the Gun

Books by Zoe Burke

An Annabelle Starkey Mystery
Jump the Gun

Charley Harper's Nature Discovery Books
What's in the Rain Forest
What's in the Woods

Other Children's Books
Lightning Bug Thunder

Jump the Gun

An Annabelle Starkey Mystery

Zoe Burke

Poisoned Pen Press

Copyright © 2013 by Zoe Burke

First Edition 2013

10 9 8 7 6 5 4 3 2 1

Library of Congress Catalog Card Number: 2012952556

ISBN: 9781464201615   Hardcover
       9781464201639   Trade Paperback

Poisoned Pen Press
6962 E. First Ave., Ste. 103
Scottsdale, AZ 85251
www.poisonedpenpress.com
info@poisonedpenpress.com

Printed in the United States of America

For Thomas, my leading man

Acknowledgments

I'm grateful beyond words to my agent, Anna Olswanger of Liza Dawson Associates. Her edits of the first drafts were spot on, and she put me in the capable hands of Jessica Tribble, Annette Rogers, and Barbara Peters at Poisoned Pen Press, who have been nothing but wonderful. I thank everyone at PPP, now and always.

Thanks to Elliott Joseph, who taught the creative writing class that inspired Annabelle Starkey.

My writer friends Margaret E. Wagner and Bonnie Smetts, who read early drafts, provided excellent suggestions and kept me motivated, and DB Finnegan invited me to join her in Bodega Bay for a writing retreat that proved invaluable.

My sister, Martha, has sustained me my whole life. She's the only one who has ever made me laugh so hard that I had to sit down in an elevator. In Paris, no less.

Sibby and I became BFFs when we were seven years old. She always tells the truth and she always helps, no matter what.

Meinrad's porch has provided sanctuary when I've needed it.

I'm lucky to have Darius, Jenay, Aidan, Camden, David R., David S., Gerk and Joe, Lolo and Bill, Gavin, Martha M. and Tom, Peter and Haig, Jamie and his gang, Kevin and Robert, and Matt and Julie in my corner. You all rock.

The Pomegranatians have been cheerful supporters, even on bad days.

Finally and forever, Thomas is the best back-row companion a girl could have. He makes everything better, all the time.

Chapter One

I love movies. They're my passion, my great escape. Oh, sure, my life is okay—decent job, loving parents, friends. But I've always been the Joan Cusack character in *Working Girl*, playing the good sport and faithful sidekick while the leading lady Melanie Griffith lands the great job, the great man, the great life. I'm thirty-two and pretty enough—if you ignore my big ears—and smart enough, but all I've ever landed was on my feet. Dull guys wanted to move in. Exciting guys wanted to move on. I couldn't seem to find my own perfect leading man.

When I met Mickey three weeks ago in Chicago at a national book convention, I liked him right away. He had Al Pacino eyes and a smile as crooked as Ellen Barkin's, and I don't know if you ever saw the movie, but when I looked at him I felt like I was smack dab in the middle of *Sea of Love*. It's one of my all-time favorites, full of hot sex and edge-of-your-seat danger, and I had a sudden urge to meet him in a grocery store wearing nothing but a raincoat—you have to see the movie, one of Pacino's top three.

On Sunday, during the final long hours of the convention, we were each taking a break. I was sipping coffee standing up at one of those tall, chairless tables common at convention centers. Mickey had perched his sunglasses on his forehead and was talking on his cell phone when he noticed me. I smiled. He fixed his gaze on me while he finished his call, then snapped his phone shut and held out his hand. "Mickey Paxton."

"Annabelle Starkey."

He held my hand a little bit longer than a handshake, and when he let it go, he said, "Wow."

"'Wow'? Does that line usually work for you?"

He laughed. "Don't know, never used it before."

"Try another one." I was still smiling.

"How about I tell you that I'm forty and I live in New York and I'm a sales director…"

"Whoa," I interrupted, "how about instead we start with your favorite movie."

He frowned. "Hmmm. Not sure. I guess *The Year of Living Dangerously*."

Now I laughed. "Is that a warning?"

"I hope not." He leaned toward me on the table. "I'd like to take you to Las Vegas with me. Tomorrow morning."

I set my coffee cup down and raised my eyebrows. "Um, you think I'm an easy pick-up?"

He took a step back. "Oh, look, no, I'm sorry, that's not it at all, I…"

"Well, I'm not. Buy me a drink first, before we get dangerous."

He smiled, that crooked smile. "You bet."

◇◇◇

We met that evening by the river at a quiet, upscale bar, one with overstuffed leather chairs and floor-to-ceiling windows. Mickey arrived first. He was waiting outside in front, on his phone again. "Got it. Looks like it will all be wrapped up tomorrow. They can handle the rest here." Pause. He winked at me. "Roger that. I'll stay under." He dropped the phone in his pocket and put his hand on my shoulder. "Glad you're here."

"You're 'under'?" I asked.

"What?"

"I heard you say that you'll 'stay under'?"

He put his hand back in his pocket. "Oh, that. Yeah, I'm under the gun, so to speak, to make sure some deals go through. You know, sales."

I did know. I was the publicity manager for a San Francisco publisher of how-to-live-your-life and here's-what-you-should-think books. But before I could ask him more about these deals, he smiled and directed me to the door, his hand on my back. "You look wonderful." We walked into the bar.

By the time we finished that first drink, I was a goner. This man was not only gorgeous—piercing brown eyes, thick, dark hair, that mischievous smile—he knew how to listen. I was nervous and talking so much that I even told him all about my cat, Bonkers, and how he likes to take baths. Mickey had me believing that he was interested in everything I had to say.

We left after the second drink. Mickey hailed a cab and I climbed in, but he didn't. "I'll pick you up at your hotel tomorrow morning. Nine sharp. We're going to Las Vegas."

"But what about the gun?"

He flinched. "What gun?"

"The one you're under."

He laughed. "Oh. I can handle that remotely. Cell phone. No problem. See you in the morning. Sleep tight." Then the cab took off and Mickey walked the other way down the street, while I watched him out the back window. He hadn't even kissed me.

You should know that I had never done anything this adventurous, ever. Except for the time a few weeks before the Chicago trip when I called in sick at work four days in a row while I went to three movies a day. My decision to trust Mickey was mostly a gut thing—though I had never been to Vegas before and had always wanted to check it out. Mickey was a true gentleman. I already felt comfortable with him. I was ready to step out of my life and right into *A Touch of Mink,* hoping things would turn out as well for me as they did for Doris Day, and that my chance meeting with a stranger would change the course of my life, too.

My alarm was set for 7:30, but I woke up at 6:00 with a herd of buffaloes—right out of any classic western movie you can think of—stampeding around my stomach. I am used to them waking me up when I'm nervous. They're kind of like annoying friends whose loyalty is so reliable that you overlook the fact that they usually make you feel nauseous.

I took a shower and washed my hair, dried it, and styled it with lots of goo and gunk. It's cut pretty short, but not as short as K. D. Lang's. By the time I finished messing with it, I looked like I could be a band member with Kiss if I just applied a lot of heavy white makeup and black eye shadow. So I took another shower and washed it again, dried it, and fluffed it up, silky and natural looking, like a healthy Catholic girl. Then I took another shower and let it air dry and put on a hat. I look good in hats, and this was a cute little cloche, like the one Angelina Jolie wore in *The Changeling*, only red. It did a good job of hiding my oversized ears—they're the main reason I have a lot of hats. I've tried longer hair, but it's straight and fine and my ears poke through it without any problem at all.

At 8:30, I went downstairs and checked out, then sat down in the hotel coffee shop and ordered a double espresso and a corn muffin and picked up a *Tribune* someone had left behind. I was reading the funnies when Mickey walked in. He smiled. "Nice hat."

Even now, when I think about Mickey, I have to catch my breath. I told him on the plane to Las Vegas, when he reached over and held my hand—which, in case you didn't know, is about the sexiest thing a guy can do—that I'm not a woman who suddenly gets on airplanes with handsome men that she's known for less than a day. He said, "Hmm! You think I'm handsome!" I must admit, though, that I did somewhat keep my head. When we got to the Chicago airport, I insisted on buying my own ticket. I didn't want to come off as a version of Julia Roberts in *Pretty Woman*, although she did end up with a great wardrobe, not to mention Richard Gere.

Our plane landed in Las Vegas right on time—which I took as a good sign, since I had never landed on time anywhere in my life—and it was a quick cab ride to the Strip. I noticed Mickey checking his phone a lot, and he looked around at everything all the time—walking through the airport and standing in the taxi line. He even looked out the back window of the cab a few times on the way to the hotel.

I touched his knee. "I'm thinking I should be calling you John, instead of Mickey."

He frowned. "And that would be because…?"

"You're acting like you're on the run, like Johnny Depp playing John Dillinger in *Public Enemies*. Did you see it? Got lousy reviews, but I loved it."

He chuckled at that, grabbed my hand, and kissed it.

Mickey had booked us a suite at the Royal Opal Resort, and we checked in around 2:30. Like I said, this was my first trip to Las Vegas, and I've got to tell you, I don't ever want to go back. The glitz, the kitsch—it's not a city, it's an amusement park where people lose their life's savings. The scope of the hotel made me more than a little uneasy. It took about thirty minutes just to find our room—first fighting our way through the gaming tables and then walking down endless halls to wrong elevator banks until we found the right one. We rode up surrounded by mirrors and Frank Sinatra singing "Fly Me to the Moon" and, at last, got off on the eighteenth floor and walked into the suite. Big bed, big basket of fruit, big mirror on the ceiling above the big bed, big screen television, big bottle of champagne.

Mickey dropped his bags, looked around, smiled at me, and said, "Hold on. I'll be right back. Got to go to the lobby for a minute."

He was out the door as fast as Matt Damon in any of the Bourne movies you can think of. The buffaloes in my stomach started grumbling—I was nervous. Maybe I had made a mistake. I thought about calling my friend Cassie again. She was housesitting Bonkers, and I had left her a message on my home answering machine the night before—she didn't use her cell phone much—telling her I was off to Sin City with a complete stranger. Maybe I'd reach her this time.

Cassie liked to be in charge and never hesitated to say, "I shouldn't tell you what to do, but here's what you should do." She was strong, with a physique toned by running the hills of San Francisco and regular yoga classes. She could be intimidating, and she knew it. Once she even told her boss to stop bossing her around because she had work to do. He fired her, and she asked me, "*Now* who's going to run that place?" Cassie was indomitable, and I loved that about her.

I tried her again at my apartment, and then on her cell phone. No answer.

But I told myself not to panic. If Mickey was a psycho, he could have raped and murdered me in Chicago. I popped the bottle of bubbly and poured two glasses, then started munching on grapes. I opened my suitcase, wondering if I should unpack, but I didn't want to appear too eager, so decided not to. I took off my hat and then opened and closed all of the drawers in the desk and the bureaus and the cupboards by the bar, inspected the stationery, read the Guest Services manual, flicked the wine glasses with my finger to see if they resonated, forgetting that I should have done that when they were empty. Then I swilled down the contents of one glass, and tapped that glass again. Yup. Good stuff. Both the glass and the bubbly.

Several minutes went by, probably about twenty. I drank the second glass of champagne and started to feel queasy. Mickey was taking his time. Was he some sort of gambling addict? Should I go find him? But what if he came back while I was looking for him? I could leave a note. Now my nervous buffaloes started stampeding again. Here I was in a movie, all right, but it wasn't *Sea of Love*. It was starting to feel more like *An Affair to Remember*, when Deborah Kerr never meets Cary Grant at the top of the Empire State Building because she gets hit by a car.

I called Mickey on his cell phone, but he didn't answer, so I left him a message—"Hi, um, where are you, anyway?" Then I tossed back my third glass. I was drinking the champagne too quickly, and it was making me burpy as well as drunk. I decided to lie down for a bit. The buffaloes drowned in the champagne, and I dozed off. I was dreaming I was riding on a train in the mountains, the train shimmying back and forth, when suddenly I was awake, and this potatohead guy was shaking me and yelling at me, "Yo! Bea! Bea! Show some life, why don'cha!"

I didn't know who this jackass was. I jumped off the bed and grabbed the nearest deadly weapon, which happened to be a hotel ballpoint pen.

"Who the fuck are you and why are you in my room?" I pointed the pen at him. I hoped I sounded a lot braver than I felt.

"Hey, get a grip. I'm a friend of Mickey's. He wants you should come with me."

"Yeah, well, I want I should stay here. Now get out." I thrust the pen toward him but I was swerving and trying to back up at the same time. My legs weren't working too well—turns out that knees really do knock in moments of terror.

"Aw, lady, if you don't come with me, you're gonna put me in a spot, and I don't like bein' in no spots." Then he pulled a gun out of his pocket. I dropped the ballpoint.

I had never seen a gun up close before. Actually, I had never seen a gun before, except on TV or in a movie. I didn't like it. He wasn't pointing it at me yet, but he had started tossing it back and forth from one hand to another. Grinning at me. His teeth were yellow and a little crooked. I was suddenly very sorry that I had followed gorgeous Mickey Paxton to Las Vegas and that I had drunk three glasses of champagne. I had to pee. Badly. That's when I thought, *Ah! Maybe I can get away from this prick!*

"Fine," I finally squeaked. "I'll come with you. But first I have to…"

"Yeah, yeah. Just hurry it up."

I grabbed my purse and started toward the bathroom door, but the fat, ugly creep put his hand on my arm to stop me and grabbed my purse. "Nice try, Bea." He took my cell phone and put it in his pocket, then he fished around some more until he found my hard plastic glasses case. He turned it over and studied it, then dropped it back in. He gave my purse back to me. Then he went into the bathroom, pulled the phone off the wall, and tossed it into the suite. "Now, like I said, hurry it up."

I figured that once I was in the bathroom, I could crawl out of the window and escape. It wasn't until I walked in and closed the door that I remembered the window was probably ten times suicide-height up from the ground. So after I peed I turned on the water in the sink and washed my face and hands and brushed my teeth and swallowed three aspirin, one at a time, from the bottle in my purse to ward off any champagne headache. Then I sat down on the toilet and tried to think. There didn't seem to be anything to do but to go with this goombah and try to get away from him once we were in the casino. I stood and picked up my purse, looking oh so calm when I came out.

"*Vamanos*, Meatball."

He rolled his eyes and took hold of my arm. We left the suite and walked to the elevator.

Chapter Two

We got into the elevator, Goober and I—one of his hands gripping my arm and the other, I was sure, gripping the gun in his pocket—along with an old woman who had punched the down button just as we arrived. She was wearing one of the greatest hats I had ever seen. I could never wear it, slanted over to the side like it was; my left ear would have stood out like a stop sign. The elevator speakers sang out with Frank's jaunty "Love and Marriage." I quickly scoped out our other company: a man wearing a Hawaiian shirt and white loafers—he was humming along with Frank—and a fifty-ish woman who looked and smelled as though she had been drinking far more than I had over the last twelve hours. I focused on the old woman. Something about her was familiar, but the fleeting feeling was probably due her kind face. I was desperate for an ally.

"Great hat!" I said, as my hand went up to my head, missing my red cloche.

"Thank you, honey. It's a Tarcelloni."

"No kidding? God, I'd love to own a Tarcelloni." To tell you the truth, I thought Tarcelloni was a kind of pasta, but I needed to come up with a plan, and maybe talking would help. "Where did you get it?"

"Oh, dear, I bought this so long ago I'm not sure I remember. Let me see, was it at Lord & Taylor's in Chicago? Or B. Altman's in Philadelphia? I hope it stays on because I can't find my hatpin."

"Well, it looks fantastic on you. Especially the color, that pale green, it really suits your…"

"Put a lid on it," Goober growled, nudging me with the gun in his pocket.

I smiled at the old woman when she sniffed at Goober. "Well! Aren't *we* a little touchy!" Then I knew just what to do. I already had this woman's sympathies, and I had to play them for all I could. I started to sob. I wailed. I snorted and sniveled. I blew my nose on Goober's sleeve. Everyone on the elevator looked for Kleenexes and handkerchiefs, and the old woman said, "There, there."

When the elevator doors opened onto the floor of the main casino, my sobbing graduated to roaring. Mr. Hawaii, Mrs. Jim Beam, and Granny Mae gathered around, trying to calm me down. Goober kept hold of my arm while watching my every move. I was doing my best to channel Holly Hunter's Oscar-worthy cry-fests from *Broadcast News*.

"Why're you cryin' like this?" asked Mr. Hawaii.

Before I could answer, Big Goob started to lead me away from my new family of friends, telling them, "It's her kid. She misses him. We hafta go now."

"Wait just a minute, big fella, something's fishy here and I want to know what's going on," slurred Mrs. Beam.

Hawaii nodded. "Yeah, wha's goin' on?"

"He has a gun!" I blurted out.

Goober sighed and squeezed my arm tighter. With his other hand he reached into his breast pocket and pulled out a badge and flashed it. "Police work, awright? Don't let this little lady fool ya, awright? Now why doncha just go on now and enjoy yours evenins."

"Well, you be nice to her, you hear?" shouted Granny Mae. She and the others stood there while we walked into the casino.

Now I was truly scared. This guy could not be a cop. Cops show you their badges first thing and don't threaten you with guns. Goobs pushed his hidden gun into my side, and his grip was bruising my arm. The longer I was in his clutches the less chance I had of surviving. And I still had no idea what was going on.

"Where are we going? Look, you kidnap me from my room at gunpoint. The least you can do is tell me what's going on." Brave words when my legs were about to crumple in fear.

"Ya see that door over there, behind the blackjack tables? That's where we're goin. And no more noise, girlie."

Girlie. It's one of those words that throws me into a fit of rage, not because I'm a blazing feminist (even though I'm sure I should be) but because the kid who lived next door when I was growing up called me that in a little rhyme he recited over and over whenever I played outside and no one else was around:

Girlie, Girlie, Girlie Goo
Ears as big as Timbuktu
Brain is smaller than an ant's
Wears her grandma's underpants.

That goddamn rhyme always made me so mad, I'd shout at him to stop, but he never would, and I'd end up running inside. But one weekend when I was about ten, I watched a video of *Gone With the Wind,* and I kept rewinding it to study Scarlett O'Hara slapping Ashley Wilkes hard across his face, over and over again. I had never seen anything so beautiful. So the next time this kid started the rhyme, he only got through the first line and a half before I was all over him, fists flying. Mom and Dad had to peel me off of him.

He never called me Girlie again.

When Nana, my grandmother, heard my parents scold me about my attack, she secretly gave me a wink. That wink has stayed with me ever since.

Glaring at Goobs, I felt a burst of adrenaline in my legs. I stomped on his foot as hard as I could. "Fuck!" he yelled, letting me go. I took off running.

It's hard to run out of a Las Vegas casino. The exits are hidden among mazes of huge rooms of gambling machines and tables. I was running, but I didn't know where. Through the rows of slot machines, through the craps tables, through a couple of bars, past the lounge singer—he was warbling a Captain and Tenille song, if you can believe it—but I couldn't find the exit, and I didn't know how far behind me galloped the Goober. I yelled to a waiter, "How do I get out of here?"

"Everyone asks me that," he beamed. "Go down that staircase, turn left at the bottom, and after you see the betting screens for the horse races, turn right. You can't miss it." What a comedian.

I skidded down those stairs at top speed, turned left, saw the screens, turned right, and kept going. Sure enough, I saw the double doors leading to the outside. I shoved through them.

Right in front of me stood Mickey. With Goobs. Whose gun was now pointed at Mickey's head. Trying to catch my breath, I focused on Mickey's get-lost-here eyes.

He gave a weak smile. "Hi."

"Mickey."

"Look, you'd better come with me and Jake here. Otherwise, we'll both be dead very soon."

"Yeah. Okay." The three of us turned around and walked back into the casino. I probably could have gotten away. By the time Jake plugged Mickey I could have jumped into a cab for the airport and caught the next plane to Uzbekistan or Papua New Guinea. I was imagining how to do this, while Mickey was looking at me and I was looking back. Yet he seemed in control, even with the gun to his head—kind of like Bruce Willis in the death-defying *Die Hard*. In that moment, Mickey was impossible to resist.

Chapter Three

"Jesus. What a lovely getaway this is turning out to be." Mickey was scowling at me.

"Don't you talk to me, Mickey. I mean it. Don't you dare speak until I have told you exactly what I think of you and your Las Vegas pal."

I didn't find him as irresistible, now that we were locked in a big meeting room and he wasn't doing a damn thing about it. I'd been banging on the door and the walls and screaming "Help!" for the past five minutes while Mickey watched. Sure that no one could hear us, he kept telling me to sit down. I ignored him and I wore myself out screaming instead. Now I was reduced to pacing, scared out of my mind. I didn't know if I would end up dead or sold into slavery. Then I thought, okay, okay. I'm over thirty and usually they go for younger women. Dead seemed more likely.

Jake had brought us to this windowless room behind the blackjack tables and left, locking the door. Mickey was sitting at a conference table with six leather swivel chairs positioned around it and a bunch of red flowers in a vase in the middle. Cocktail napkins were stacked next to the vase, a Sony plasma TV sat on the buffet, and a full bar with a small refrigerator could serve a decent party. Big men in expensive suits had probably gathered in that room, flashing diamonds with enough carats to be a girl's holy savior, let alone her best friend.

Mickey finally yelled. "Damn it! Sit down! You might even *consider* telling me what the hell's going on!"

I spun around to glare at him. "WHAT? Are you KIDDING ME? What's going on is that I've been trying to get out of here!"

"How's that working out for you?" He glared back at me.

I grabbed a Diet Coke from the fridge and started slugging it down. I didn't want Mickey to say anything or interrupt my train of thought, because I knew the effect he could have on me, and I didn't want to lose track of how angry I was. I gripped the Coke can and pointed at him over the table. "I did not come here with you to get involved in your petty criminal schemes, and I sure hope they are petty, Bub, because I am not going to jail for your sake just because your eyes could outshine Robert Downey Junior's."

I stopped here to regroup; the Diet Coke helped. "First, you ditch me in the hotel room—just had to get to the gaming tables, right? I don't know what the hell happened to you. Then I get kidnapped by the potatohead guy, but I almost get away, until I run into him holding a gun to your head. Your *head*. Then it's up to me to save your ass, and now, here I am, with you, whom I barely know, and my life is clearly in danger, and I may never pitch another book again, let alone do all the other things I want to do with my life, like go to Paris. Boy, I must have been out of my mind to have come here with you."

At this point my throat was getting tight. As the words spilled out of me, I got more scared than angry, and I did not want to lose whatever little control I still had. I sat down across from him and shut up. Took another swallow. Took a deep breath.

"Stop."

"Don't say 'stop,' Mickey. Don't you dare tell me to stop." But I did stop because if I didn't, I was going to cry. I hate it that when you cry, men think that they no longer have to debate you, or listen to you. No, when you start crying they try to take care of you. Weak little you. So I didn't cry. I sat and breathed and stared at an imaginary spot on the wall behind Mickey, just to the right of his perfectly shaped left ear.

"Do you want to hear my side of the story?" Mickey punctuated his words like little drum beats. "Or, do you want to rant and rave at me until Jake gets back and we both end up getting killed?"

Now, I really did not like his tone. It had a little bit of Meryl Streep's nun in *Doubt* layered over my father's voice when he was telling me that I couldn't play football in junior high. "Now, Bea, there are no girls on the football team. If I have something to say about it there never will be girls on the football team, and I damn sure won't have my daughter be a linebacker for the Detroit Lions!" I was secretly pleased back then that he thought I had that kind of potential. But Mickey's condescension got me back into my rage.

"Ooohh. Give me one good reason why I should listen to a goddamn thing you have to say. One goddamn *good* reason."

He leaned toward me. "How about this: I have never seen this guy Jake before. I do not know who he is. I do not know why we are here. I do not know anything about what is going on here. Maybe *you're* the one who should be doing some explaining."

This was rich. The dumb ploy. But I wasn't falling for it.

"Oh pleeeeease. Please please please. Give me some credit. Assume I maintain a peapod of intelligence. This trip was your idea. I have never even been to Las Vegas before. And you've been acting all Johnny Depp on me. Now *I'm* supposed to explain to *you* what the hell is going on?"

"That's right! You know why?" His voice was getting really loud.

"Why!" I made sure mine was louder than his.

"Because I never knew your name was Beatrice!"

"Excuusse me?" I screamed.

"Beatrice! Beatrice! Beatrice! Beatrice!" He vocally snapped my name like rapid fire out of an Uzi, while standing and slamming his fist on the table with each word. "Listen to me!" He sat back down and inhaled. "I left our suite to pick up a little gift for you at one of the hotel shops. I came out of the store to suddenly feel a very real gun stuck in my back. It was Jake—whom

I have *never* seen before in my life—and he said to come with him, because 'my friend' was in trouble. I said, 'What friend is that?' He didn't say any more until he brought me to this room. He frisked me, took my phone, and told me to shut up and sit down. I was locked in here until he came and got me and paraded me in front of you as you were making your ill-timed escape."

Mickey was tense, so I forgave his put-down of my courageous escape attempt.

Mickey took a breath. "I asked again, when he came to get me, 'What friend is in trouble?' This time he laughed. 'Beatrice Starkey, your Las Vegas date, man. Like you don't know that.' Okay? *Beatrice?* So you tell *me* what the fuck is going on here, *Annabelle!* Or, excuse *me,* I mean *Beatrice!* Jake seems to know you, but apparently, I don't!"

This stopped me cold. I was as confused as Jane Eyre when she's about to marry Mr. Rochester and his brother-in-law stops the wedding. I stared at Mickey. I think my mouth was open.

"Well?"

"I don't know."

"You don't know?"

"Beatrice is my first name and Annabelle is my middle name. But I have no idea how Jake knows my first name. He did call me Bea when he kidnapped me, now that I think about it." I inhaled. "I go by Annabelle Starkey and hardly anyone calls me Bea, except my parents. I prefer Annabelle over Beatrice. Annabelle conjures up visions of a Southern beauty, with hoop skirts and lots of mysteries underneath them, but Beatrice sounds like a jolly fat aunt who puts happy faces made out of chocolate chips on her oatmeal cookies."

Mickey wrinkled his forehead. "So now *I* am someone without any peapods of intelligence, who is supposed to believe that Jake knows you, but you don't know him."

"Mickey, I really don't know." I managed a little smile. "But I think you probably have lots of peapods."

"You do, do you."

"Yes, I do."

"And you really don't know what's going on."

"I really don't. I've never seen this guy before."

Mickey got up from the table and started pacing around the room. He opened the refrigerator and slammed it shut again. He rattled the doorknob, even though he knew it was locked. He muttered something that sounded like "Beatrice Annabelle Starkey, Beatrice Annabelle Starkey, Beatrice Annabelle..."

"What?"

"Nothing."

I sat and wondered if I ever *had* seen Jake anywhere before, if I had ever seen a gun before, if I had ever done something so horrendous that people would kill me for it, if I had ever dated someone who had used my social security number to order arms for Al Qaeda, if I really shouldn't have gotten snippy with the woman at the grocery store check-out counter three Tuesdays before when she was talking to her friend instead of checking my groceries —maybe she was *married* to Jake—if my employer was a front for the mob (after all, I never was privy to sales figures and it was a privately owned company, and my boss always wore really expensive Italian-made shoes), if my father had finally and secretly realized his childhood dream of becoming an international spy and his enemies were trying to get at him through his family members, if government agents had intercepted that email I sent to Mom a few years ago when I proposed that George W. Bush and Dick Cheney should be exiled to a remote island and forced to watch "Judge Judy" reruns for the rest of their miserable lives.

"Mickey, did he say anything else? Was he with anyone?"

"When he took me he was alone. The gun had a silencer. He said Beatrice was in trouble. He brought me here. I said, wait a minute, who was he, why were we in this room, I just got to Las Vegas, and I started for the door. He grabbed me and conked me on the back of the head with his gun."

Mickey had stopped pacing. It wasn't until then that I realized he had been rubbing his head off and on. "Oh, god. That's... horrible...are you all right?"

"Yeah, I think so. I woke up with a big headache." He rubbed his head again.

I still had my purse with me—it's pretty big but has a long strap that fits over my head and the opposite shoulder, and it's a good style to have if you ever find yourself trying to run away from thugs in a casino—and I put it on the table and pulled out my bottle of aspirin. "Here, take about seventeen."

Mickey took the bottle and dumped four into his hand. "Thanks." He filled a glass with water at the sink at the end of the room, tossed all four pills at once in his mouth, and swallowed them with a few gulps. I'm always impressed with no-nonsense pill takers. Me, I take my daily vitamins one at a time, with about a half glass of water for each.

"Do you have a big lump?"

"Yes." Mickey sat back down at the table, folded his arms on it, and put his forehead on top of his arms.

"None of this makes sense. I know you know that already, but listen: if Jake wanted me, if he was really after me, why didn't he come up to the suite and get me, instead of taking you first and knocking you out? He could have kidnapped me easily enough without involving you at all, and, well, it just doesn't make any sense."

"That's right, An-na-belle! None of this makes a-ny sense!" Mickey kept his head down.

I'm pretty good when it comes to reading people, and I could tell that Mickey didn't want to hear squat from me. I shut up and tried to come up with more theories—did my next-door neighbor finally figure out that I was the one who picked a few of her prize tulips? God, I only took about three, and she must have had at least twenty in her garden. Her last name is O'Malley—some IRA connection? I walked over to the TV and turned it on and right off again: a Cialis commercial. I picked up the phone that was on the conference table; dead. I sat back down.

After a very long few minutes, Mickey raised his head and looked at me. I held his gaze until he shifted his eyes to the right of my bigger-than-life Dumbo left ear. My hands shot up to smooth down my hair, which was a good thing, because it was sticking out. I probably looked like Alfalfa of *The Little Rascals.* Finally, Mickey spoke. "Okay."

"Okay?"

"Okay. I accept that neither one of us knows what's going on. But I assume that you're the primary target."

"From your position I get why that would be a fair assumption."

"Thank you very much."

"Yeah." I paused. "Um, Mickey, did Jake show you his badge?"

"His *badge?*"

Apparently he hadn't. I nodded. "I guess he's a cop, or else he's pretending to be one."

Mickey brought his hands to his face and leaned back in his chair. I focused on my empty Diet Coke can and rolled it around in my hands. Eventually I looked back at him. He was staring at me, puzzled. I bit the inside of my lower lip and was about to study my can some more when he said, "Hey. Let's work on getting out of this, shall we?"

Then he did a very nice thing. He reached across the table and put his hand over mine and gave it a squeeze. I don't know why he felt so kindly toward me just then, but perhaps he had at last noticed my flying nun ears and felt sorry for me. Whatever his reasons, in that moment he was my Mr. Rochester. He wasn't puffing up his chest, he wasn't taking charge, and most of all, he was trusting me. He made me feel like we belonged together in this thing, whatever it was.

"Mickey?"

"Yes."

"You really are a very nice guy."

"Annabelle?"

"Yes."

"Are you related to Ringo?"

"Nope."

"Do you have any other ideas why someone might want to kidnap you, or worse?

I laughed. "You mean besides being related to Ringo?"

"Just a thought."

"No, no ideas. But I did like Ringo the best of the Beatles. I've always been attracted to a nose you can count on."

Mickey felt his nose and we both laughed.

"Okay," he said.

"Mickey?"

"Yeah."

"Whatever I might have done to get you into this, I am sorry."

He nodded. "I wonder how come I still think you are so beautiful?"

Probably because you haven't noticed my ears yet. Instead I said, "Because I am telling you the truth. And the truth is always beautiful." He smiled at that. I wanted to ask him what gift he had bought me, but at that moment Jake walked in.

Chapter Four

When I was five, I went to the circus with my best friend, Ethan, and his parents. The featured attraction was the "tallest giraffe in the world," and when Ethan's dad told me this, I said, "Oh, really!" It was the first time I had ever said such a grown-up thing, and I felt old and wise beyond my years. *Take me anywhere*, I thought, *a circus, a cocktail party, you name it, I can talk to grown-ups*. Actually, I couldn't wait to see this giraffe, but either Ethan's dad got it wrong or the giraffe had another engagement, because he didn't show.

When I got home from the circus, I was so tired I went right upstairs to lie down on my bed. As I drifted off to sleep, my mother called me to dinner. I knew I should go downstairs to eat, or I'd be in trouble. But my eyelids got heavier and heavier. Her voice got softer and softer. When I woke up, it was morning.

It had been quite a day. I had started using grown-up talk, and I had defied my mother: my first steps toward independence.

When Jake said, "Hey, lovebirds, we'll be leavin' here in a coupla minutes. There's a car waitin' outside," the first words out of my mouth were "Oh, really!" and I suddenly flashed on that day. I concentrated on Mickey's eyes when I said this, and he stayed fixed on mine.

Then he said, "Just where are we going, Jake?"

"That's somethin' for me to know and you to find out, huh!"

I said, "Huh.…Why don't you take us to see the world's tall-est giraffe?" Now, this didn't make sense, but I was stalling and, once again, talking was all I could come up with.

Apparently Mickey was doing the same thing. "Yeah, Jake, why don't you take us to see the world's tallest giraffe?"

"You two are somethin' else. You talkin' crazy cuz you're afraid? Is that it? I don't know nuthin' about no giraffes, and even if I did, I wouldn't take yous to see 'em. Now get up and come with me. We're leavin'."

"I can't leave—" I was still transfixed by Mickey's peepers— "without knowing where I'm going."

Jake sniggered, a nasty, phlegmy sound. "Right. Like you're makin' the rules here. Like I care what you want here. Now stop talkin' and makin' goo-goo eyes at each other. Let's go."

I didn't move. Neither did Mickey. And we kept staring at each other. "Jake, if you shoot us here, because we won't go with you, I bet whoever you work for will not be too happy. I bet whoever you work for doesn't want us dead, because if whoever you work for did want us dead, you would have already killed us. So we know you're not going to shoot us. Tell us where we're going. Maybe we'll cooperate." This was Mickey talking, cool and collected, like he talked to psycho maniacs all the time.

"I work for me, not some boss. I ain't gonna shoot you, wise ass, but I can crack your head again easily enough…"

"And drag us through the casino to your waiting car? All by yourself? Come on, Jake, you aren't that stupid. Tell us what's going on."

He really might be that stupid. Stupid is as stupid does, as Forest Gump would say. But I followed Mickey's lead. "Yeah, Jake, either tell us or take us to see the tallest giraffe in the world."

"Cut out that giraffe shit. Both of yous shut up." Jake walked behind me as he said this, and right then I shoved my chair back as hard as I could into his overextended belly. He lost his balance and fell down. I was up like a shot and sat on his chest while Mickey dove to the floor and grabbed Jake's arms. Jake tried kicking his feet but they were tangled up in the chair legs.

"Dental floss!" I yelled.

"What?!"

"Dental floss! Dental floss! It's in my purse!" I always have a super-size floss dispenser with me. I'm convinced that leafy greens get stuck in between my teeth more than anyone else's in the world.

Jake was big and squirming. I was having a hard time staying on top of him. Mickey repositioned himself to straddle Jake and lean over his head, while still holding his arms down. For a moment we were riding a one-humped camel over a bumpy desert. I raised myself up and grabbed my purse off the table, fished out the floss, and climbed under the table to tie Jake's ankles together. He was still kicking and squirming, and I couldn't manage it. Then I heard a crack, and an "Ooof!" and the legs slowed down. I pulled out and wrapped several yards of the stuff around his ankles and tied them to the leg of the conference table, which weighed about a ton. When I emerged from under the table, Jake had blood all over his face, and Mickey had blood all over his hand.

"Is he dead?" I gasped.

Mickey shook his head. "Not even close. I broke his nose."

Jake began to wriggle again. I moved up to his wrists and Mickey held his arms well enough for me to wrap the floss around and tie it. Then we managed to roll Jake over on his side and push him so that he was lined up between two of the table legs, and I tied his wrists to the second leg.

Jake was yelling now, so I stood up and grabbed a bunch of napkins from the table and jammed them in his mouth. "Shut up, Jake! Just shut up!"

I picked up the vase and turned it upside down, splattering him with flowers and water.

Mickey stood up, panting, and studied Jake, who was red all over from blood and daisies. I was shaking; Mickey seemed calm. He walked to the sink, washed the blood off, and dried his hands on more napkins. Then he went back to Jake, knelt down beside him, and felt in his pockets.

"No phones. He must have ditched them." He stood up. "Let's get out of here, Beatrice Annabelle." I picked up my purse and followed him to the door.

When we stepped into the casino, no one took any notice of us. Mickey held my hand and whispered, "Let's walk calmly and normally, like nothing is going on. Let's not draw attention to ourselves. We don't know if any of Jake's friends are around." I gave him a sporting smile, and then I saw a side door and sprinted for it, pulling Mickey with me. We tore out of there like racing cheetahs, dashing across the street and away from the casino. We hailed a cab that was coming out of the hotel's front driveway. It didn't have its light on, but it stopped anyway.

Mickey opened the back door for me, and I was about to get in, when I stopped. "Oh!"

"What? Get in!"

But someone was already in the cab, and it was Granny Mae, the Tarcelloni hat lady.

"Hello, dear!" She smiled sweetly and beckoned to me. "I asked the driver to stop—you both seem to be a bit frantic. Please get in. I'm happy to share the taxi with you." Her hat was on the seat beside her. She picked it up and moved over, holding her hat on her lap.

Mickey nodded. I jumped in while he ran around to the other side and piled into the cab, out of breath.

"Where to?" asked the driver.

"Police station. The nearest one."

I was so happy to hear Mickey say those words.

"You two all right?" the cabbie asked, looking at us in the rear-view mirror.

"We're all right. Thank you."

"Señora, do you want me to drop you off first?" We were idling at the curb.

Tarcelloni started fidgeting with the brim of her hat, clearly upset. "Oh, dear. This could be a problem."

"Mickey, this is, uh, what is your name?"

"Doris Stonington, dear. What is yours?"

I looked at her, a little breathless, and suddenly choked. I knew her, not only from the elevator encounter, but from before. But Doris Stonington? That wasn't her name. Speechless, I studied her face. *Mary.* That was it. Mary something.

Mickey frowned at me and then answered Mary. "This is Annabelle Starkey, and I'm Mickey Paxton."

"Pleased to meet you, Mr. Paxton. Annabelle, dear, what a lovely name!"

"Oh, thanks, yes…"

"Look," said Mickey, "I don't mean to be rude, but we were on the way to the police station, remember? And we're in a hurry, remember? And what exactly are we doing now?" He sounded a little bit edgy.

The cab driver's cell phone rang. He put the car in park and took the call.

"Mickey," I started slowly, still looking at Mary, "Doris was very kind to me on the elevator when I was abducted."

"Abducted? But he was a policeman!" She reached over and patted my hand.

"Well, he wasn't really a policeman, *Doris*. He pulled out that badge, but he couldn't have been a policeman because he took me from my room at gunpoint."

"Well, dear, this is very distressing. Have you called your son? He must be worried about you."

"Your SON? You have a SON?" Mickey turned in his seat as best he could to look at me across Mary.

"No, no, no, Mickey, I do not have a son. Really, I don't. Doris, please, I can't explain all of that now."

At this point the cab driver hung up and turned around in his seat and faced all of us. "Excuse me for interrupting, but do you want me to take you somewhere, or do you want to sit here with the meter running while you all chat back there?"

"Hold on for just a minute, please. Don't go anywhere yet. Now, Doris, tell me, what is going on? You seem very nervous, and you're going to ruin your Tarcelloni if you keep twisting the brim like that." I glanced at Mickey, who was scowling at me.

"Well, it's a bit embarrassing, I'm afraid. You see, I love to gamble—I made a bundle at the Royal Opal, by the way! But my family doesn't approve of my pastime—they call it a nasty habit, in fact—and so I came to Las Vegas without telling anyone, and I was planning on staying at another hotel tonight, hoping they wouldn't find me."

"Ms. Stonington…" started Mickey.

"Please, dear, call me Doris."

"Fine, Doris. None of this is any of our business. Why don't we drop you off and then we'll go to the police?"

She let go of her hat and clasped her hands together. "Well, I hadn't really decided yet where to spend the night, you see."

Mickey sighed. "You can ride with us if you like, and then the cab driver here, I'm sure, would be happy to take you wherever you wish, won't you, sir?"

"If the señora has the ample fare, I will take her anywhere." Apparently this guy's day job was writing poetry.

"Well, I could do that, I suppose…" Mary gave Mickey a tiny smile.

"Good! Fine! Great! Let's get out of here!" Mickey was as antsy as Woody Allen. The cabbie put the car into gear and started to step on the gas.

"Well, except there is just one little problem," I said.

The cabbie braked. Mickey gaped. "What! What! What!"

"Can I talk to you for one moment, outside?"

Mickey looked like he was going to explode, but I held his eyes and he finally said, "Fine," and opened his door.

The cabbie sighed, put the car back in park, leaned against his door, and stretched his feet out on the front seat. "Meter's still running, amigos."

Mickey and I both got out of the cab and walked around to the back. "This date of ours is getting weirder and weirder," I started.

He barked a sarcastic laugh. "You think?"

"I know her."

"Yes, you've already made that clear, that you saw her in the elevator, and yes, it is really weird that she stopped for us, but…"

"No, Mickey, listen. I know her. From before. She lives at Tall Oaks, a nursing home in Santa Rosa, where Nana, my grandmother, lived. Sometimes when I'd visit she'd be sitting in the lobby and we'd say hello, mention something about the weather, stuff like that. I don't know much about her, but…" I paused.

"But…?" Mickey's jaw was clenched.

"Her name isn't Doris Stonington. It's Mary something."

Mickey stared. "You've got to be kidding me."

"I wish."

He leaned against the trunk of the taxi and looked back down the Strip. "Do you think she recognizes you, from there?"

"I don't know. She might be up to no good, but she might be crazy. At Tall Oaks, Nana lived in the Alzheimer's wing. I don't know where Mary's room was, but maybe she has some sort of dementia. Maybe she really thinks her name is Doris. Maybe she doesn't remember me at all from before. But she seems very lucid. My grandmother wouldn't have even known how to hail a cab, let alone find her way around Las Vegas."

Mickey thought for a moment. "So how'd we end up in the same cab as a woman who knew your grandmother?"

"Yet another question for us to answer."

"Or not. I'm not sure I care very much about the answer. I do care about getting out of Las Vegas before I get hit over the head again."

"Look, Jake knows who I am, and now Mary is here, and maybe she knows who I am, too. I say, let's play dumb for a while and see what we can find out. We can ask her some questions on the way to the police."

Mickey rubbed his face with his hands. "All right. Let's go."

We got back in the cab and shut the doors. I felt a little chill when I noticed my purse had been moved. I had left it on the seat, I was sure, but now it was on the floor. I picked it up and put it on my lap.

Mickey glanced at the cab driver's ID pasted on the back of the front seat. "Luis? We're ready." Luis turned to put on his seat belt when Mary piped up.

"Actually, I'd rather not go with you. Why don't you let me out here, and you two go on without me. I hope everything turns out all right."

This time I patted her hand. "You'll stay with us, and then Luis will take you to the hotel of your choice, remember?" I smiled at her. *"Mary?"*

Turned out I couldn't play dumb. Mickey sighed.

She jerked her head around to face me. "Mary? No, dear, I'm Doris, and…"

"Cut it out, Mary. We know each other, remember? From Tall Oaks. I recognize you now. You dyed your hair, didn't you? Nice highlights, by the way. Anyway, now we're all going to have a nice little chat."

Luis shook his head at us in the rear-view mirror. He started to put the car in drive but stopped when Mary protested, "But you don't want to be seen with me. The police are looking for me."

Luis groaned. Mickey and I both yelled, "What?!"

Mary sighed and focused on her hat in her lap. "I'm on parole. I was in jail. I took someone else's money and gambled it away. When I got out my family put me in that old folks home in Santa Rosa. I've been living there for six months. I ran away." She paused. "It's possible that recently some people at Tall Oaks have discovered that they are missing some, well, valuables, you might say."

Mickey groaned. "Great. A thief. Really great."

Luis stroked his chin and muttered, "Oh boy."

I opened my purse and looked for my wallet; it was still there. I sat back in the seat. "Jeez."

"Okay, here's what we're going to do." Mickey took charge, manlike. "Doris, or Mary, or whoever you are, I want you to answer two simple questions, and then I am going to decide who is riding in this cab and who is not."

Even in the midst of my mind-numbing confusion, there was a little tiger voice in my head saying, "Yeah, so who made you king?" But I let him continue.

Mary was still. "All right, Mr. Paxton."

"What is your real name, and why shouldn't we turn you over to the police right now?"

Mary spoke calmly. "My name is Mary Rosen." She gave me an apologetic smile. "I was hoping you wouldn't recognize me, dear." She turned back to Mickey. "You don't want to turn me over to the police because one of them just kidnapped your lovely Annabelle."

The cab driver jerked to attention and squinted at me in his rear-view mirror.

"He probably wasn't a policeman," I said.

"You don't know that for certain, dear."

All I did know for certain was that Mary did not have Alzheimer's. She was making too much sense.

We needed a plan and, I figured, a change of scenery. My stomach growled. I flashed on *Heat,* with Pacino and DeNiro. The cop and the thief meet at a restaurant and talk amiably about how they won't hesitate to kill each other. Not a great movie, but I liked how cool they were.

"Food," I said.

"Food?" Mickey sort of shouted.

"Food. Let's go somewhere and eat something and decide what to do."

Luis turned in his seat toward us. "We should go somewhere, anywhere, amigos."

Mickey took a deep breath. "Why don't you take all of us to a coffee shop. One that's out of the way. We clearly have some sorting out to do."

"Sure thing." Luis put the taxi in gear and eased into traffic. Mary looked straight ahead. Mickey and I traded glances, and then I turned to the window. It was dusk, and the lights of the Strip were coming alive while we headed away from them, their colors brightly flashing and offering no solace at all.

Chapter Five

When I was in my mid twenties, Nana started showing all the signs of dementia. Physically, she was still in great shape. She was only seventy, still driving, keeping her own house, tending her garden. But she repeated herself all the time and forgot how to do simple things like turn on the oven. She got lost more than once while running errands, calling my mother and saying alarming things like, "Honey, where am I supposed to be right now?" She never got nasty and antagonistic, which was a blessing, but instead slowly slipped into another reality that had less and less to do with our own. Mom and Dad moved her into Tall Oaks about two years later and though at first she didn't like it and kept trying to leave, she eventually grew used to the place and I could tell she felt safe there. That was the most important thing. Tall Oaks is a ritzy place as far as retirement homes go. The residents range from the super wealthy to the comfortably middle class—Nana was decidedly of the latter group. The rooms are large and can accommodate the residents' own furniture, so they feel as much at home as possible. I liked most of the staff, and the nurses seemed to be especially fond of Nana.

Nana was my best friend in the world while I was growing up. She didn't bake cookies and knit afghans, but she did drive me to my Brownie meetings in a big Pontiac convertible—top always down, even in winter—taught me how to dance, recited poetry and memorable lines from famous plays, knew enough about plumbing to fix leaky kitchen sink pipes, and played a mean game of Crazy Eights. When her illness overtook her, I faithfully visited her each Sunday, driving north from my apartment in San Francisco over the Golden Gate Bridge into Sonoma County and Santa Rosa. Sometimes she knew who I was and sometimes she didn't, but she was always glad to see me. Occasionally we would watch movies on TV. Other times I would read Ogden Nash poems to her—they always made her laugh—and Robert Louis Stevenson's *A Child's Garden of Verses*, which she gave me when I was six. We'd sing together, too, old standards. She could remember her favorites, like "Lullaby of Birdland," even when she could remember nothing else.

Nana died in her sleep a couple of months before I flew to Chicago for that book convention. My parents were vacationing in Europe when it happened, so I arranged for her furniture to be put in storage, and I packed up the few personal things she had at Tall Oaks and took them home with me—some clothes, a few baubles and scarves, and an old pendulum clock that hadn't worked ever since I could remember. As Luis drove us to the coffee shop, I teared up, missing Nana terribly and remembering Mom's heartbroken face when I gave her the clock and the rest of Nana's things.

"Here we are." Luis pulled up alongside an all-night eatery adorned with the neon message, "The Full House: Where You Don't Have to Get Lucky to Get a Good Meal."

"Seems fine, Luis," Mickey said. "You want to join us inside or wait for us in the cab? I'd like you to stick around, if you can."

"Coffee sounds good, but the meter is running, you understand?"

"How about this. I'll buy you a meal, and I'll pay you $200 plus the current meter charges, plus any additional meter charges that we incur once we leave here. Sound fair?" I had noticed that money didn't seem to be a problem for Mickey. He wore designer sunglasses, he overtipped, and that suite, well, I figured he had to be one helluva salesman.

"Bueno. Let's eat." Luis turned off the engine and the four of us entered The Full House. It was not full. It was nearly empty.

We slid into a big booth, looked over the menus—which offered everything anyone could ever want, from all-day breakfast to steak dinners, with juice, milkshakes, and booze—and ordered. I chose a garden burger and stuck with Diet Coke, Mary ordered a bourbon on the rocks, Luis got coffee and a three-cheese omelet with a side of bacon. I was a little more than disappointed when Mickey ordered calamari. Ick.

When the waitress walked away, Mickey started. "So, this is how I think our situation sums up. Annabelle and I are being chased by a thug or thugs…"

"You mean that fake policeman?"

"Mary, if you don't mind, I would like to just lay out the situation before we get into a big discussion." Mickey was sounding a little tired.

"Fine, Mr. Paxton. I understand." The waitress showed up with the drinks, and Mary proceeded to down her bourbon just as dramatically as Bette Davis did in *Whatever Happened to Baby Jane?* She motioned to the waitress for another. "Please go on."

"Thank you. We've been kidnapped and assaulted. The police are looking for Mary, we think Annabelle and Mary have some nearly forgotten past in common. Luis here had the misfortune of picking us all up in his cab and finding himself involved in our various getaways."

Luis poured some cream in his mug. "Misfortune? Tonight I am a rich man." He slurped his coffee.

"Whatever. Now, we don't know who is after us or why, and we're not sure if the police really are hunting for Mary. And, the question I have to ask is this: is there a connection between our two situations?"

"Mr. Paxton! I may be a thief, but I assure you, I do not keep company with thugs." Mary seemed appalled.

I jumped in. "Mary, you have to see this from our point of view. I mean, I got kidnapped and ran into an acquaintance of my grandmother's, who's evading the law, all in a matter of hours—well, actually minutes." I looked at Mickey. "But it does seem unlikely, nevertheless. Mary doesn't know anything about me. She was at Tall Oaks the last few months or so that Nana was alive. You know, Mary, come to think of it, I hadn't seen you there for the couple of weeks before Nana died. To tell you the truth, I figured you had passed away, if you'll pardon my saying so."

Mary smiled. "I broke my foot. I was reaching for something and fell. It was a bad break, and I was in rehab for quite a spell."

"Well, anyway, Mickey, Mary and I only had a passing acquaintance. I'd see her in the lobby and say hello. That's all."

Mary's second drink had shown up, and she took a big gulp. "Well, dear, that's not quite all."

"Oh boy, here we go again." Mickey leaned back against the booth and rolled his eyes up at the acoustic-tile suspended ceiling.

"I don't like your tone, Mickey, I really don't."

"My *tone,* Annabelle? Here's what I don't like: not knowing what the HELL is going on!" Mickey obviously had control issues.

"Oh, my, please stop, the two of you, please. It's just that I remember something that Annabelle doesn't." Mary took another swallow.

"Annabelle doesn't seem to remember things well at all, I'm coming to learn!"

"I remember things just fine, Mickey! Usually, anyway! I mean, I forget my keys sometimes, and I lose sunglasses regularly…But I'm not a flake and I've been completely honest with you. And right now you should just let Mary talk!" I took a slug of Diet Coke, to calm myself.

"Yes, if you don't mind, Mick, chill, and let her continue," Luis joined in.

Mickey shook his head and continued eyeballing the ceiling.

Mary swallowed the last of her second bourbon and cleared her throat. "I used to sit with Annabelle's grandmother in the afternoons. The nurses let me visit the Alzheimer's wing every day—it's a secure wing, Mr. Paxton, so that the patients don't wander out and get lost—and I became very fond of Nana. I read to her sometimes. She was very sweet. Sometimes she thought I was her sister."

I smiled. "Really? Phyllis? Did she call you Phyllis?"

"Oh, no, I don't think so. I believe she called me Sara."

"That was Phyllis' daughter, my mother's cousin. Phyllis was Nana's sister, and Sara's mother. So Sara was actually my first cousin once removed. They lived in Omaha, and sometimes…"

"Annabelle!" Mickey interrupted.

"Okay, okay."

Mary continued. "One day I was still with Nana when Annabelle came into her room. I introduced myself then, and we had a lovely conversation."

Everyone sat there for a minute and stared at Mary. Finally Mickey snapped, "That's it? That's the whole story? That's the extent of the secret past of Doris Stonington a.k.a. Mary Rosen and Beatrice Annabelle Starkey? You once had a lovely conversation? This really clears things up."

"Mr. Paxton, I never said anything about solving any problems. I merely was reminding Annabelle about the full extent of our previous encounters. I do apologize if I have disappointed you." Mary sniffed.

Mickey shut his eyes. "I am merely trying to get to the bottom of things, and we seem to have reached another dead end."

"No, we haven't," I said. Mickey swiveled his eyes and raised his eyebrows at me. "I remember that lovely conversation now. Mary told me about her son. Didn't you tell me about your son, Mary?"

"Well, now, dear, I don't remember exactly what we talked about. I could have told you about my son." Mary reached up and patted her hair gingerly.

"Why is this important?" Mickey gave us what he probably thought was a smile, but it was really a grimace.

"Because, Mickey, Mary's son's name is Jake. And as I recall, he was a football player."

"My goodness, dear, you do have a fine memory after all!"

I kept my eyes on Mickey until he said, "Jake?"

"Jake."

Mary chimed in. "Why, yes, Jake!"

Luis frowned. "Nice name."

"Can we assume he's a big man, Mary?" Mickey asked.

"Oh yes, quite big. Actually, it has been quite a while since I last saw him, but I think I can safely assume that he is still big."

"Yes, I think you can assume that." Now I started fidgeting with my hair.

"Finally, we're getting somewhere," said Mickey.

"Really! We are? Do you know Jake?" asked Mary.

"Jake held us at gunpoint tonight."

Mary smiled, which I thought was truly an inappropriate response. A shriek or an incredulous gasp would have made more sense. But instead, she sat there grinning, as goofy as Ruth Gordon in *Harold and Maude*.

"This is amusing to you, Mary?" I suddenly didn't like her very much.

"The man on the elevator with you was not my son." She shook her bourbon glass, rattling the ice cubes. "The last I knew, he was in jail."

"Aha! So he's a convict, too! Why am I not surprised? Why was HE in jail?" Mickey leaned toward Mary over the table.

"Well, Mr. Paxton, for the same reason I was. He's a gambler, and he got in too deep and couldn't pay off a loan, and he ended up killing someone."

At this moment Luis was taking another swallow of coffee and he coughed and sprayed it over his plate. He wiped his mouth. "Sorry. Went down the wrong pipe."

I set my hand on Mary's shoulder. "You said you were in jail for stealing. So that's not the same reason Jake was in jail. I mean, murder is not stealing." Why was I trying to help her out, even though I felt like I was going to barf?

"I didn't say anything about murder. It was self defense. He went to his bookie to explain about the money, and the bookie came at him, and Jake hit him on the head and the man died. But he got sent to jail anyway on second-degree murder."

Luis no longer looked like he considered himself a lucky man. He scanned all of us through a Clint Eastwood squint. After a few moments, during which we were all silent, he spoke. "What's next?"

The waitress showed up balancing plates on her arms and began distributing them. Mickey slouched down, frowned at his plate of fried calamari and pushed it away, unfortunately in my direction. I scrunched up my nose and pushed it back.

Luis and I started eating. I was ravenous, which was not unusual. Stress always makes me feel like I need to bulk up a few pounds. Mary picked at Mickey's calamari. While I was on my third mouthful of veggie burger, Mickey coughed and straightened.

"Mary, I don't trust you. Annabelle, I'm trying to trust you. But I need answers. So, here's what's next. We're going back to the hotel to get Jake, and we're going to make him tell us what is going on."

Mickey stood up. I swallowed, grabbed his arm, and gave him my best you-have-to-be-out-of-your-mind look: jaw dropped, eyes wide and blinking. "Uh, I don't *think* so! I do *not* think that is a good idea!"

"Chances are, Annabelle, that Jake is still tied up with your dental floss. And don't you want to know what the hell is going on? He's our best source of information."

"Yeah, but what if he's not still tied up, and he has friends with him, bad guys, and they all have guns? We'll all be dead or kidnapped."

"Not likely. I think we'll be just fine."

"Oh really? Why?" I shoved the last of the veggie burger in my mouth.

"Because first of all we're not even sure that he has any friends. And second of all, because we've got Mary with us. Jake won't hurt his mother, will he, Mary?" Mickey turned to her. "If we all go and see Jake, will he hurt you and us?"

"Oh, I couldn't say, because he's not my son." Mary shook her head back and forth.

Mickey shrugged his shoulders with a you've-got-to-admit-this-sounds-like-a good-plan expression. I stood up, still chewing, and managed to ask, "What if Jake *isn't* Mary's son?"

"It's the only connection we have!"

"Yes, but she really didn't recognize him on the elevator."

"Annabelle, smarten up here. She's faking it. She's lying now and she was faking it then. At least consider that possibility."

"Okay. And you have to consider the possibility that he's not her son."

Luis whistled. "We are back to zero, my friends."

Mickey threw money on the table for the bill. "Let's get out of here."

"And go where?" I grabbed a handful of French fries.

"I don't know. Let's just get the hell out of here."

"I'll stay here, Mr. Paxton. There's really no need for you to concern yourself with me," said Mary.

Mickey glowered at her. "Are you kidding me? I don't trust you past my little finger. If you *are* Jake's mother, and I mean the Jake that we know, you could be setting us up, calling him to come find us."

"But you don't have to tell me where you're going."

"Lady, you've got Luis' medallion number memorized, I bet. I don't want you putting Luis in danger, or us. So we're sticking together for a while. In fact, forget the hotel and Jake. Let's take our chances with the police station. Back to plan A. How does that sound?" Mickey looked at me.

"Sure. Let's go." I had no reason to trust Mary or go out on a limb for her.

Luis got up, but Mary refused. "Please, don't do this. I cannot go back to Tall Oaks. Surely you can tell by now that I don't belong there. I am fully independent, I am not demented, I do not need caregivers. My family just stuck me in there as a way to keep track of me. I am not trying to harm any of you in any way."

I was ready to leave her there at this point, too tired and confused to save anyone but myself...and maybe Mickey. But then the roar of a car charging too fast into the parking lot and car doors slamming caught our attention. Out the window we spied Jake and another guy hustling toward the restaurant.

"Holy crap," I said. All of us, including Mary, frantically sought a way out of the diner.

Luis shouted "There!" and pointed to a back door with an exit sign. We ran out faster than you can say pigs-in-a-blanket. As luck would have it—we were in Las Vegas, after all—Luis had parked near our exit, far from the entrance. We piled in, Mickey took the front seat this time, and Luis tore off.

Mickey whirled to glare at Mary. "Was that your doing, Mary? Did you call Jake and tell him where to find us? Did you?"

Mary didn't answer, but I stated the facts. "She never left the table, Mickey. She couldn't have called him."

Mickey turned back around. No one said anything else. Luis kept driving, and lucky for us he knew what he was doing. He made lots of sudden turns, getting us out of the city, and drove fast on the straightaways. After a few minutes he slowed down. "We're fine, now."

It was plenty fine with me that where we were going was up to Luis. Frankly, I expected him to take us to the police station, but he drove for about twenty minutes, a ways out of Las Vegas and into another town, some nowhere place in the middle of the flat desert landscape. The small, ranch-style houses had asphalt or ground red rocks for front yards. I figured each one had a kidney-shaped pool behind it. Not much vegetation. Only a few cars on the streets. It was the last place in America I would want to live. "Wow. Who could live here?"

"Me, for one," said Luis, and I shut up. A few minutes later he pulled in front of the lobby of the Sleep Tight Inn, turned off the engine, and swung to Mickey on his right. He pointed at the meter. "You owe me this much plus two hundred bucks, Mick."

Mickey pulled out his wallet and counted out the money. He handed it to Luis, and then wrote something on what I figured was his business card, saying, "This is who I am. All of my information is there."

Luis stuck the money in his pocket while he was reading Mickey's card. He glanced at Mickey and they traded a nod. Then Luis turned to see all of us. "Now, here's what I'm going to tell you, folks. You don't want to go to the police. You want to stay here for the night. We lost them back there at the diner, and I'm going to park my cab somewhere away from here and away from my house, in case they're looking for it. You should be safe tonight. But stay in the motel, and don't leave."

"Luis, what are you talking about? Why shouldn't we go to the police?" Mickey spoke very softly, asking as if he didn't want to hear the answer.

"That hombre back there, the big one with the bandage on his nose? That's the one you know as Jake?"

Mickey and I nodded and Mary said, "He was the man on the elevator, but without the bandage..."

"Mickey broke it when we escaped," I explained.

Luis sighed. "He's a cop. A real one, and a bad one, but he's in good with the department. I don't know what's going on here, but I know that if he's threatening you with guns and shit, then it ain't pretty, and I'd bet he really does want to kill you."

We were stupefied by this piece of news. Mary said, "Yes, well, he did have a badge."

"Luis, how do you know this cop? Have you had trouble with him before?"

Luis looked at me. "Sure, and maybe I'll tell you about it. Right now, I want to ditch my cab and ditch all of you, okay? Stay here tonight. Get some sleep. I'm going to think about all of this and see if I can come up with any ideas. I'll be back in the morning, or I'll call you."

This wasn't very reassuring, let me tell you. Until that moment, we didn't know anything about this Luis guy except that he was kind and trying to help us. Now we found out he had a history with Jake. Maybe Jake wanted to kill him, too, or maybe Luis had committed some crime and that was the trouble he was talking about. Here we were, stuck in the middle of yet another inexplicable coincidence, heading for more danger.

"Let's go. Mary, come on. Annabelle." Mickey seemed to think this was the best thing to do, like we could trust Luis, and I agreed to do what I was told—not a typical response on my part, but taking direction well is something that comes in handy during a crisis when you can't tell the difference between a cop and a thug, a sweet old lady and a thief, and a man who is in the process of stealing your heart and a man who could be landing you in a deep, unmarked grave in the middle of the Mojave desert. So I got out of the cab.

Chapter Six

The Sleep Tight Inn was nothing like an inn. It was a motor lodge. A cheap and simple motor lodge with a small outside pool and a little coffee shop. Mickey, Mary, and I walked up to the registration desk. The check-in clerk's nametag read Lorinda. Her poofy blonde hair and heavy black eye makeup reminded me of Karen Black in *Five Easy Pieces*.

"One room, two beds, please," said Mickey.

I tugged on his sleeve and mouthed, "One room?"

"I'm not letting her out of my sight."

"You're in luck, sir. We have just one room available. There was a wedding in town, and it was a pretty big one, and we got booked up."

"Two beds, right?"

"Yes sir. Forty-eight dollars."

"Fine. We'll take it." Mickey reached for his wallet and brought out an American Express card.

"Sorry, sir, we don't take Am Ex." Mickey tried a VISA card next. "Uh, sorry, sir, but the expiration date on this has passed. Do you have a replacement card?" Mickey took the card back and pulled out cash. "Yes, sir, that should do nicely." Lorinda gave Mickey the registration form and he filled it out in his name only, Michael T. Paxton. I made a mental note to ask him what his middle name was, at the appropriate time.

"One key? Or two? Or, uh, three?"

"One," said Mickey, but I elbowed him. "No, make that two," he added.

She rummaged in the drawers below the counter. "Gee, I am sorry. It looks like I only have the one. If you'd like to wait, I can look..."

"We'll take the one, that will be fine." I snatched the key and the three of us walked outside and down the row of rooms to number 46. The room looked like just about every other hotel room I had ever stayed in, except, of course, the Royal Opal, with the big everythings, which I had not actually stayed in, overnight, anyway. Nope. Instead I was here. With my date. And a friend of my grandmother's.

"I don't suppose there's any bourbon in this room," Mary wondered out loud.

"No mini bar that I can see." It's usually the first thing I look for in a hotel room. It's good to have emergency rations on hand at all times, like a can of Pringles potato chips and a cold beer.

"Well, then, I will just prepare for bed." Mary disappeared into the bathroom. She left her purse on the floor by the door.

Mickey picked it up and quickly rifled through it. He pulled out her phone and turned it on. "Damn. It's locked. Probably needs a password." He sat down in one of the two chairs situated by the window with a table between them, and dropped the phone on the table.

I sat down on the edge of the bed nearest to him. "What are you thinking?"

"I don't know how else Jake would have found us, unless Mary contacted him." He took a deep breath. "But right now, I'm tired of thinking and I want some rest." Mickey was under a lot of stress, but so was I for heaven's sake, and I figured we were a team in this, we had to stick together, we had to man the lifeboats, save older women and children first, throw our lives on the line for the sake of god and country. Well, something like that. And I wasn't ready to sleep.

"Are you still thinking that this is all my fault?"

"Had I not met you in Chicago and asked you to come with me to Las Vegas, none of this would have happened. That is what I am thinking."

"Which means you think it is all my fault, right? Just say it!"

"Circumstances have arisen because we made this trip together. That does not mean that I think you contrived the circumstances."

"Oh. Well, I still feel like I should be apologizing to you, but I don't know what for."

"Then don't. Believe me, I am not waiting for an apology, or expecting an apology. I'll let you know if I think you owe me one." He was looking at me when he said this, but I bent my head slightly and focused on my shoes, which were my nice red wedge sandals. "So, Annabelle, what are you thinking?"

"I'm thinking that my toenails need clipping." I kept looking at them.

"Ah." He moved from the chair and sat next to me on the bed. He put his arm around my waist and he kissed my cheek, like a good friend would do, like your best friend in high school who just happened to be a boy. "I want to tell you something."

I turned to face him just as Mary came out of the bathroom, and Mickey and I stood up like teenagers caught kissing in the rec room when they are supposed to be playing ping pong. "Who's next?" she asked cheerfully as she made her way to the other bed.

"Um, that would be me." I went in to attend to myself the best I could, what without a toothbrush and toothpaste. I hunted for my contact lens case in my purse until I remembered I had packed it in my toiletries bag, swore, and then filled each of the two plastic cups on the sink counter with water, popped out my lenses, and put one in each cup. You're not supposed to do this—apparently lenses can absorb bacteria from the water and infect your eyes and make you blind—but my eyes were itching like crazy from the dry air, so I took the risk. I retrieved my eyeglasses from the case in my purse and put them on, combed my hair to no great effect, peed, and rinsed with some mouthwash that was in a little Listerine bottle next to the little "Desert Flower" shampoo bottle. When I came out of the bathroom, Mary was lying on the other bed with the cheap fake-quilt spread over her, her shoes and jacket off, and sound asleep. I knew she was asleep because she was snoring.

I looked at Mickey. He smiled, got up, and as he passed me to go into the bathroom, he stroked my arm with his hand. "Nice specs."

"Don't drink the water in the cups. They have my lenses in them."

I put my purse on the floor under the empty bed, hoping Mary wouldn't crawl around down there looking for it. What should my next move should be? Lie down next to Mary, sit in one of the chairs, sit on Mickey's bed—which is how I was already thinking of it—lie down on Mickey's bed, gaze out the window at the parking lot like I was lost in thought, do sit-ups—I never do sit-ups, but I could make a good impression that way—better yet, do push-ups? I opted to sit on the end of Mickey's bed—he had, after all, told me that he wanted to tell me something—and turned on the television. I pressed the mute button so as not to disturb Mary. When Mickey emerged, I was bathed in the TV light and glued to the scene near the end of *Silverado* when Kevin Kline and Brian Dennehy face each other in a gun duel. It's one of my favorite movies; I've seen it at least six times. The lack of sound did not diminish my understanding of the plot. But when I looked up and saw Mickey standing there shirtless, shoeless, and sockless, the cowboys became immediately less appealing.

"Hi," he said.

"Hi back atcha."

He sat down next to me and looked at the television. "*Silverado.* Another of my faves."

That canceled out his penchant for squid. "Me, too."

Then he picked up the remote and pushed the power button and the screen went black. He put his arm around me again, and kissed me. On the lips. Soft. Just the right length of time. Eyes open at the beginning, closed at the end. I was looking at him for the whole kiss. No tongue. Just full lips. Nicest lips I had ever felt. He pulled back and his eyes scanned my face, looking for something specific. He brought his right hand up to the side of my face and tenderly touched the scar on my left cheek. "Where did you get that?"

"Car accident. Sixteen. Thirty stitches. Skidded on the ice in Omaha when we went there for Christmas vacation." We were both whispering, Mary was still snoring. He leaned over and kissed my scar. Then he took off my glasses, folded them, and put them on the bedside table. I'm telling you, he was doing everything perfectly. "Mickey."

"Yes."

"What did you want to tell me?"

He moved back from me slightly and met my eyes full on. A knowing smile crossed his mouth. "All through this entire crazy, insane, ridiculous, somewhat terrifying day, I have not been able for one moment to lose the feeling I had when I first saw you in Chicago, that you are the most beguiling woman I have ever met. In spite of everything that's happened, I want to be with you, I want to know you." Then he kissed me again. Soft again. Just lips again.

I didn't believe him, really. I know that I'm pretty, except for the ears, but so many women are more extraordinary than I am, and Mickey, given his movie-star looks, must have dated most of them. Also, I know he didn't want to be with me when he was hit over the head by Jake or when he thought I was lying to him about, well, everything. But I liked hearing this anyway, and I wanted to be with him and know him, too. He had a cagey side, which could mean bad news for me. But deep inside I didn't believe that anything going on was his doing, and I really liked it that he was sticking around instead of ditching me at the Sleep Tight Inn. Sure, maybe he just wanted to figure out the truth about the day's events, but…that kiss. It was the real deal. I smiled, a big smile, and put both my arms around him, turned on the bed slightly so that one leg was bent on top of it and I was facing him, and I planted my mouth on his, and kissed him hard, and he kissed me back hard, and this time we found our tongues. Mickey reached underneath my t-shirt and started to undo my bra.

"We can't do this," I whispered.

"Oh, yes we can." He popped the clasp as deftly as Kevin Costner undid Susan Sarandon's in *Bull Durham*. I gasped.

"No, no we can't. Mary is in the next bed. We can't risk waking her."

"We won't." He pulled my shirt over my head and drew my bra down off my shoulders. He looked at my breasts. "We just have to be very quiet." Then he gathered me in his arms and laid me back on the bed.

"Very quiet," I agreed.

"Very. Silence is golden."

And several minutes later, when I felt that my head and heart would explode with pleasure, I kept my mouth pressed against his as my body shuddered. And he managed to move without making the bed creak.

Like I said, he was perfect.

We fell asleep with my head on his chest and Mary snoring away. I don't remember dreaming anything. I was lost in a deep, delicious sleep. As the first light of morning came in through the window, I woke up in the same position I had fallen asleep in. My first thought was that Mickey's arm was probably going to be numb for the next twenty-four hours after it had been underneath me for the last six. I gently moved away from him and turned over to face Mary's bed, hopeful that the feeling in his arm would return and we wouldn't have to make an emergency trip to the hospital to have it amputated. I was drifting off again to sleep when I noticed something, and sat up with a start. "Oh!"

Mickey awakened quickly and sat up himself. "What! Hey! What!"

"Mary's gone." I put on my glasses.

Mickey looked. "So much for not letting her out of my sight."

"Yeah." I paused. "What if something bad happened? Maybe she was taken…"

Mickey shook his head. "If someone had come in here we would have heard them. We locked the door, they would have had to bust in." We both looked at the door, and, of course, the chain lock was no longer hitched.

"Maybe she got up and walked outside, and then something happened."

Mickey jumped out of bed and pulled on his pants, went to the door, opened it a crack, and looked outside. "She's not out here. I suppose she could be in the coffee shop." He shut the door and peered at the table across the room. "Her phone is gone."

I leaned over the side of the bed and looked under it.

Mickey chuckled. "What are you doing? You're about to fall on the floor."

My purse was still there. I grabbed it, sat up, reached in, and pulled out my wallet. "Phew. I think she rummaged through my purse in the cab." Then I sat up. "We still don't know if Mary is in on whatever is going on or not. Hell, Mickey, we don't even know if she's dead or alive at this point." I shivered.

"Hey," Mickey sat down next to me on the bed. "Let's get cleaned up and wait to hear from Luis, and decide what to do next." He kissed the top of my head. "Take a shower."

I kissed him and got up. On my way to the bathroom, I turned to him. "How's your arm, by the way?"

"What arm?" He smiled at me.

I walked into the bathroom and shut the door and gave a little yelp. Mary had drunk my contact lenses.

Chapter Seven

Luis called and showed up about ninety minutes later at the coffee shop. He slid into the booth and motioned to the waitress to bring him a mug. "So, Mary's gone." Mickey had already told him this on the phone. "And if someone took her, that means someone knows you two are here as well." Mickey and I had thought of that already, too, which is why we were in the coffee shop. Safety in numbers.

"Luis," I said, "we've been talking, and we're now convinced that Mary *is* involved with Jake. I think she was waiting for him in your cab, when she saw us run out. She must have phoned Jake and told him the cab number or license plate or something… except he must have still been tied up at that point."

Luis shrugged. "She probably texted him. I don't remember her calling anyone from the cab, anyway."

The waitress, Jackie, was busy serving a few tables of hungover people from the wedding, but managed to bring a mug to Luis. Mickey picked up the copper thermos on the table and poured Luis a cup, followed by another one for himself. I was watching Jackie get back to her ailing customers, making a mental note to leave her a big tip, when I wondered, who in the world gets married on a Monday? This was Tuesday morning. But then I heard one of them talking about the wedding "on Sunday" and figured that a lot of them had stayed over for at least another day.

Mickey sipped his coffee. "Right, Luis. So maybe now you can fill us in. Who's Jake? What do we need to know about him? Why is he after us?"

"I don't know why he's after you. Like I said, he's a bad cop. I know this because I'm a cop. On suspension."

Mickey and I both gave a little start at this piece of news. I reached my hand under the table and put it on his leg, for my own reassurance.

"His real name is Chuck Lowery. He's been on the force for about ten years. He's a bruiser, a guy who cares only about being in charge. He likes power and he likes to prove to people that he's powerful. He used to beat up kids after he'd arrest them for smoking a joint."

Luis paused and shook his head as he looked across the room at a couple of bleary-eyed revelers. "He'd have no problem, for instance, coming into a place like this and yanking that poor kid up by the back of the shirt and smacking him around after accusing him of being on drugs, even though it's obvious that the guy is just hung over."

The thought of Jake coming in here and yanking anyone to their feet didn't start my day off with a bang.

"Why do you think he told me his name was Jake?" Mickey asked.

"And why do you think he was hanging around the Royal Opal and trying to kidnap us?" I added.

"Chuck is tied in with some high rollers. He hangs at the casinos a lot. I think he gets paid on the side for being a bouncer for some of them. Look, I made a couple of calls to some of my friends on the force. They told me that nothing new is going on that they know about. Chuck's up to his usual shit, but that's all I could find out. He got the Jake nickname a little while ago when he had trouble with one of his victims, and this guy slit the side of his nose, just like Jack Nicholson got it in *Chinatown*."

"Jake Gittes." Mickey and I both recited Nicholson's character's name in unison. We looked at each other.

"Maybe Mary wasn't lying," I said.

Mickey shook his head. "I don't know. I don't think we can trust anything Mary told us." Then he took a swallow of coffee. "Okay, so why not go to the police? Will they all rally behind him? Can't we bring charges?"

"Sure, you can, but you might end up dead if you do that. Like I said, he is tied in with some big names in Las Vegas, and they won't put up with anyone messing with their boy."

"Are you talking about the mob?" When I asked that I suddenly left my body. I mean, how would I ever be in a situation when I was seriously asking someone about mob connections?

"No, not like you mean. Just a local Vegas mob. But still very dangerous."

I started playing with the salt and pepper shakers. These are important tools for reducing tension, in case you didn't know. Twirl them around, dump some salt on the table, make designs in it with your fingers, really, there's a multitude of things you can do.

Mickey and Luis watched me for a minute until Mickey coughed and I stopped.

"Luis," he said, "why are you here? Why did you come back for us? Hanging out with us could be dangerous for you, right?"

Luis nodded. "Right. But I hate this guy. He's the reason I'm on suspension, and he's the reason I'm driving a fucking cab in Las Vegas. He's the reason my wife doesn't want to leave the house. I want to figure out a way to bring him down."

"What did he do, to get you suspended?"

Luis gazed across the room again, then turned back to us. "I caught him stealing money off a corpse. Not a drug-dealer corpse, mind you. An *abuela,* an old lady who had just won a jackpot. She got hit by a car. She was dead. And this piece of shit robbed her. And he saw me see him, and he put me up against the wall and said if I told he wouldn't come after me, he'd come after my wife. And when I got home that night, Ruby was crying. He had called her a few minutes earlier and told her that I was dead. That she was a widow, and he'd be visiting her real soon. I held her and told her what had happened, and she calmed down. But the next day when she went to work, Chuck followed her there, and when she left, he followed her home. He did that for a full week. She was terrified."

Luis stopped and took a sip of coffee. "So one day in the squad room I lost it. Jumped him, all the while screaming that he was a thief. The guys pulled me off him before Chuck had a chance to take a swing. I got suspended. Two months."

"No one believed you?" Mickey asked.

Luis shook his head. "I've got no real evidence, and he's been around longer than I have. Now I'm spending as much time as I can following him, trying to nail him. So far, all I have is a lot of photographs of him coming in and out of casinos." He paused. "I'm working weekends as a private security guard at a casino off the Strip, but mostly I'm driving a cab, filling in for a friend. Even now, once a week, Chuck comes by and parks outside my house for about an hour. Just sits there. Ruby's a nervous wreck. She took a leave of absence from her job and rarely goes anywhere."

I sat on my hands, rather than play with the salt again, and my left leg started bouncing as my heel began a fast tap on the floor. Mickey put his hand on my knee and sat up straight, his other hand clenched in a fist on the table. "Jesus, man, don't you have anyone on your side?"

"My partner's doing what he can. Keeping an eye out. Look, Lowery is ruining my life. I need to fix this, and whatever mess you two are in might be the way for me to get him."

Oh, great. Just what we need. Someone who wants a shoot-out with Jake or Chuck or whoever at the OK Corral. "Luis, sorry if I'm being rude here, but why don't you just move to another city, work for another police department?"

Mickey answered me quietly. "Luis is no coward."

"Oh jeez," I said. "I didn't mean to imply that. But Ruby's scared out of her mind, and it sounds like it could be impossible to bring Jake down."

Luis sighed. "I want to get him. I want to expose him. I've been trying to come up with the right plan."

"And that's us?" I paused. "I'm sorry for your troubles, I really am, but I don't think we can help you. We don't even know why we're mixed up in this, and right now I'm thinking, let's get the hell out of Las Vegas. Let's go to the airport, now, let's go. Okay, Mickey?"

He didn't move. I reached for my purse and turned toward him, indicating that he should slide out of the booth, but, again, he didn't move. "Annabelle, when did Nana die?"

I didn't get it, but answered. "A couple of months ago."

"Mary knew her, Jake is probably Mary's son, we think he's after you, her granddaughter. I wonder if..."

"...something bad happened to Nana? You think he *murdered* her?" My stomach wound itself into an instant knot. I picked up my water glass and drank in huge gulps. When I put the glass back down my hand was shaking.

Mickey put his hand on top of mine. "Sorry. Just a thought."

I took a few deep breaths. "I don't know why anyone would kill Nana. She didn't have much besides her house, and my parents sold that in order to afford Tall Oaks. But Jake did hurt an old lady..." Something was adding up, but to what, I had no clue. How could all of this have anything to do with Nana? "What do you want to do, Mickey? I'm sensing more and more that this is my situation, not yours, so don't you want to leave town?"

"I'm the one who was knocked out. I've got a stake in this. I can't walk away from it."

"Don't go all Gary Cooper on me." I was mixing up *High Noon* with the OK Corral, but you're allowed to do that in frightening situations. "You don't have to be a hero. Let's get out of here."

"What if something happened to Nana, something bad? Don't you want to find out?"

I wasn't sure if I wanted to find out or not. "We can find that out in California better than we can find it out here. Come home with me, we'll drive up to Tall Oaks, ask some questions."

Mickey considered this, then frowned. "What about all our things at the hotel? My laptop? It's got all of my business stuff on it."

This bothered me. I mean, I was willing to let go of the six pairs of shoes I had brought to Chicago, and my new Donna Karan raincoat, and, oh yeah, *my* laptop with all of *my* business stuff on it. But I had the distinct impression that Mickey was coming up with reasons to stay, so that he and Luis could face the enemy rather than head for the hills. Me, I was all for running.

Luis said, "Amigos, let's go back to the hotel, get your things. I'll notice if anyone is watching or following us. Then I'll take you to the airport. I promise. No fare." I was about to say "What's not fair?" when I figured it out.

Luis and Mickey waited for me to give in. I was outnumbered and suddenly exhausted, so I nodded my agreement, thinking to myself, *my god, Annabelle, you are an idiot.* We left the coffee shop and headed for Luis' taxi. But when Mickey opened the back door, a dark blue sedan screeched into the parking lot and pulled up next to the cab.

Two men poured out and yelled, "Police! Don't move! All three of you! Stop there!" They had guns. So we stopped, with our arms in the air.

"Line up against the cab there, hands on the roof, spread eagle," one commanded, and so we did, while they patted our legs and hips and sides and arms to see if we had any guns or other weapons, I guess. We didn't. They pulled Mickey's and Luis' wallets out of their back pockets and fished out their licenses. Then they grabbed my purse and rifled through it, finally finding my license. They took a look at all of the IDs and then handed them back to us. They calmed down.

"Okay turn around." We did.

"What's this all about?" I tried to sound calm while expecting Jake to show up any minute. Mickey apparently had lost his voice.

"We're looking for a Mary Rosen, and we got a report that this cab was seen picking her up last night on the strip."

Somehow all of this search and seizure had rallied my strength and made me a little—no, a lot more than pissed off. And that anger was feeding my voice. "You mean that we are dangerous criminals because we are using the same cab?" I didn't like these guys much. Mickey was still silent.

"We have reason to think the lady was kidnapped. We are taking all precautions. Which is why I would like to hear from the cab driver here if he remembers her, and if any of you are connected to her in any way."

I saw Mickey steal a look at Luis, and Luis shook his head, just the slightest bit. I thought about lying and telling them that I had never seen or heard of Mary Rosen in my entire life. But if these guys were good cops and not Jake's buddies, and if Mary really was a criminal, then that lie could land me in a Las Vegas slammer for obstructing justice. And one rule I live by is that when in doubt, either say nothing or tell the truth. I said nothing.

Mickey obviously had a different rule book. "We don't know the woman and we can't help you. Luis drove us around all night last night, and we never picked up another passenger. In fact, I paid this man a two-hundred-dollar tip for the privilege of chauffeuring me and my girlfriend, isn't that right, Luis?" With this Mickey put his arm around me and smiled like he and I had been together for years. I, on the other hand, looked at him like he was out of his mind.

The policemen turned to Luis for confirmation, and Mickey took the opportunity to whisper in my ear, "These guys are not cops."

I didn't know how he knew this, but I had about half a second to decide whether to trust him or think he was crazy, and if I thought he was crazy, or leading me into danger, what would that have meant about our night together? So I trusted him, and before Luis could open his mouth, I said, "That's right. We're here on a kind of romantic holiday. Some friends got married on Sunday, and we decided to stick around for a couple of days after the wedding. Luis turned out to be the perfect driver." I smiled at Luis.

"So, Mr. Maldonado, what's your story?"

"I could not have picked up any lady last night since I was with this couple from about six on."

"Then how do you explain the report that your cab was outside the Royal Opal last night and Mary Rosen was seen getting in it?"

Luis thought for a moment and came up with an answer. "I wasn't driving this cab last night. I drove my own car, it's nicer, and these people wanted a nice evening. I left the cab in the street. Perhaps someone took it for a joy ride?" I didn't think this explanation was going to fly, but if these guys really weren't police, and they were only looking for Mary, then any explanation would do.

"Where did you park the cab?" one of them asked. The guy with hair. The other guy was bald. They didn't wear uniforms or hats.

"On Locust Street, not far from my house."

"Was it there when you got back last night?"

"I didn't look last night, but when I went to get it this morning, it was there."

"All right," Baldy said. "Give me your card. We may want to get in touch with you again." Luis reached in his pocket and pulled out two business cards, one each for Moe and Curly. Then Moe turned to us. "Are you staying at this motel, just in case we need to contact you again?"

Great. Do we make this up, too? See what I mean about telling the truth? When you don't, you just have to keep making more stuff up.

Mickey answered. "No, in fact we're leaving today for San Francisco. But let me give you my card with my cell phone on it; feel free to call me." Mickey patted his pockets and then shrugged. "Sorry, I guess I'm out. I'll write it down on Luis' card."

Moe handed him the card and gave him a pen. "All right, thanks, Mr. Paxton. Ms. Starkey. Hey, you're not related to Ringo, are you?"

I shook my head and groaned. "You wouldn't believe how often I'm asked that."

Moe and Curly got back in their Buick and drove away. I turned to Luis and Mickey. "Would either of you like to clue me in here?"

Luis answered. "They're not the police. I gave Mick a signal and he picked up on it. Nice to be working as a team." He nodded at Mickey and Mickey nodded back. Man stuff, I guess.

"How do you know they're not the police? Do you know every single cop in these here parts?" I was starting to talk like a cowboy, but there was some male-bonding thing going on, and I got sucked in.

"No, I don't," Luis said. "But I saw the bald-headed one's revolver, a Smith and Wesson .38. It's not a gun that any policeman on duty would carry. And, I didn't recognize them. And, their shoes were wrong. They were fancy leather, with thin soles." To tell you the truth, this last statement made the most sense to me. I'm a firm believer that you can judge a person by his or her shoes. I looked at Mickey's feet and was relieved to see that he was wearing a nice pair of Cole Hahn brown casuals: stylish, but not flamboyant; practical, but not clunky; masculine, but not macho.

"Okay," I said. "So let's get the hell out of Dodge." Mickey and Luis each had a slight smile as I turned away from them and walked back to the cab. I hoped they'd notice I was swaggering a little. I turned around to face them. "You know, if those guys weren't cops, and they're looking for Mary, then Mary is hooked up in something bad, and probably *is* connected with Jake. And we really don't know anything about her at all and we can't trust her at all. And we're still in a lot of trouble."

"Yes. All true. We don't know who we can trust, except each other." Mickey patted Luis on the back.

"Well, Mickey, we could trust a United Airlines pilot, couldn't we? How about we go to the airport and trust one of them to get us to San Francisco? How about we skip the hotel escapade, compadre?" It was really hot and my glasses were slipping down on my nose and I was pushing them back up as I posed this very logical question.

Mickey walked up to me and touched my cheek. My scar. "If we go to the hotel, we might be helping Luis. We'll make it quick, I promise. And then, as you say, we'll get the hell out of Dodge."

His touch alone would probably have been enough to make me agree with him. But something else was holding me there. That gut thing again. A little-voice thing. Maybe a macho thing. I couldn't let go of the idea that Nana could have been murdered. I was getting in touch with my inner male. "Luis," I said, "Let's go to the Royal Opal. One hand shakes the other, my friend."

I have no idea, really, what I meant by that. But Luis and Mickey were kind enough to let it slide, and we all got in the taxi and headed for the Strip.

Chapter Eight

Las Vegas really is hell on earth. At about 11:00 in the morning the temperature felt like seven hundred degrees. Without my contacts, I could measure the heat by the rate of speed at which my glasses flew down my nose. Plus, I had been wearing the same clothes for far too long, my hair was plastered to my head like a bathing cap—and I had no hat to hide under—and I was developing some sort of rash—a heat rash, no doubt—right at my waistline where my pants buttoned. While my right hand was busy pushing my glasses up my face, my left was scratching around my navel. Luckily I had on my favorite pink T-shirt and my Levis because I look good in them, but at this point they were stretched out and wet and probably smelled.

Mickey and Luis were quiet, and I started thinking about the two of them in the front seat, while I sat in the back. Why do the men always assume the front seat is theirs? Then I remembered that I had gotten in the cab first and had chosen the back seat, and come to think of it, I was more comfortable back there, as comfortable as I could be in Las Vegas. Apparently, they haven't invented air conditioning cold enough for that wasteland. Either that or Luis' cab's AC needed a rebuild. I was hot and itchy and it was just as well that no one was sitting very near me. Luis, for some mysterious reason, did not seem to be sweating. This is as weird to me as people who eat whatever the hell they want and don't gain any weight.

I was looking at the back of Mickey's head. Nice shape. Nice thick hair, black with some gray starting to show up. He told me that first night we met in Chicago that his mother had been a hair stylist and his father, a plumber. He was an only child and his parents doted on him and saved everything they could to put him through college. A real American story. But they were killed in a car accident when he was twenty-five. I thought about that, staring at his head, and my eyes filled up.

He was looking for a stopgap job after college when he got into publishing. He found out he was good at sales and stuck with it. Sales people in publishing—and probably in any business—make the most money. Editors don't make squat, unless they handle acquisitions for megapublishers and have their own imprints. It used to be that a sales rep could sell a blockbuster to Barnes and Noble and put his kid through college on that order alone. Okay, I might be exaggerating, but not by much. All of that was changing, what with e-books and iPads, but Mickey prepared well for that and was scouting for new opportunities. I wasn't sure what that meant. Anyway, he didn't have any kids, he had only himself to support, so for the time being he was sitting pretty, financially. Physically, too, as I've already stated.

Luis pulled up in front of the Royal Opal. "Here we are. How do you want to do this?"

"Nothing special," said Mickey. "Let's just go up to the room and pack, and then come down and check out, and we'll keep our eyes open for anything."

Luis said, "Okay." Mickey turned to me. I didn't move. I didn't want to move. I sure as hell didn't want to go back into that hotel. This was a very bad idea and I should have insisted on going to the airport. But Mickey and Luis started getting out of the car, and I didn't want to stay there by myself. I didn't want to do anything by myself right then. So I opened the back door and stepped out. Mickey shut the door and took my hand.

Luis told the bellman that we'd be right back and tipped him so that the taxi could sit there for a while. We headed toward the elevators—a straight shot this time—and breathed a sigh of relief when the doors shut after us. We got out on eighteen and walked down the hall to our suite. Mickey pulled the key card out of his wallet, opened the door, and we walked in.

My stomach lurched. Not from buffaloes this time. Just pure fear.

The place was ransacked. Trashed. Furniture turned over. Drawers turned upside down. The fruit basket—which, when I was kidnapped by Jake, had a couple of mangoes, a pear, and lots of strawberries left in it—had been stomped into a gooey mess. The bed looked worse than the morning after the most raucous night of sex I could ever imagine, with the sheets and blankets and pillows all balled up and on the wrong ends. The pictures had been removed from the walls. The stupid little hotel safe had been busted open. My clothes were thrown all over the place. Mickey's, too. It looked like the wake-up scene in *The Hangover,* but there was nothing funny about it.

I lost it. I started shaking so hard I sat down on the nearest sittable thing, which happened to be the coffee table, tipped over on its side. I was hyperventilating and crying at the same time. Apparently, Mickey and Luis didn't think this response was inappropriate. They simply let me sit there and shake and cry. Mickey went back to the door and engaged the dead bolt. Luis opened closet doors. Then they started drifting around the room like homeless people, picking through stuff, holding up a sock here, a belt there, and dropping the items back on the floor. Eventually they came over and sat on the couch and just kind of watched me. I guess it was a shock thing.

When you lose it like that, you only have so much to lose, and then it is lost, and you can breathe again. This happened to me. I suddenly took a deep breath, wiped my eyes, and swallowed hard. "We should get out of here, right now."

Mickey reached his hand out to my knee. "Whoever did this is gone. Let's get what we need and then split."

"To the airport, right?" He squeezed my hand. "Right."

So I got up, went over to a pile of my clothes, picked up my khaki pants, a white t-shirt, and clean underwear, and headed for the bathroom. I stripped, got in the shower—even though it had only been about three hours since my last one—stood there for as long as it took for my shoulders to unhunch, turned off the water and dried myself, and got dressed. That's when I realized I had picked up Mickey's khakis instead of mine. They were comfy and not so tight around my waist, and that could help the rash situation, so I kept them on and rolled up the legs so I wouldn't trip on them. I combed my hair straight back, wet, cleaned my glasses and put them on, and walked back out into the suite. I found my SF Giants baseball cap, put it on—bill forward—and sat down with Mickey and Luis. They hadn't moved an inch.

"Okay," I said. "I'm ready."

Luis got up and headed for the bathroom, and I could hear him running the sink water. Mickey patted my knee. "You will never be able to say that I was not an exciting date."

"No, I will never be able to say that. Now change your clothes. Maybe put on your khakis."

Mickey stood up, leaned over, and kissed me. The bill of my cap hit his forehead. He turned it ninety degrees and kissed me again. "I'll be right back, and then we'll get out of here."

A feeling of panic filled me. "Where are you going? The last time you said you'd be right back, you were not right back!"

Mickey tilted his head toward the bathroom. "I'm going in there to change my clothes, okay?"

"Okay. But before you do, there's something I've been meaning to ask you."

"Okay, shoot."

"My present. When you left me in this suite before, you were getting me a present at the hotel store. What was it?"

Mickey hit his head in an oh-right, now-I-remember motion and came back over to me and sat down. He reached in his pants pocket and brought out his hand in a fist, holding it toward me. I opened my hand flat out and held it underneath his. He let go of his fist and a small brown object fell into my hand.

I examined it closely: a beautiful animal, carved out of some rich brown stone. "A mountain lion?"

"Yes. It's a fetish."

"It's wonderful. I love it. Does it mean something special?"

Mickey laughed then. "Yeah, in fact part of Mountain Lion's power is to protect you while you're traveling."

I laughed, too. "I'm not so sure he's doing a very good job."

"That depends on your point of view. You're still safe so far, aren't you?"

"I can't argue with that. Do you give mountain lion fetishes to all your first dates?"

He put the palm of his hand on my cheek. "Never before. I saw it in the shop window when we came in. I collect them."

I gave Mickey a kiss, and he got up and sorted through clothes in a pile on the floor. I watched him find a t-shirt, socks, and boxers, and search for a pair of pants. He finally grabbed his jeans. Then he stood up and kind of looked me over. He turned my cap back around. "Nice pants." We laughed. Luis came out of the bathroom, and Mickey went in.

I had no reason to think it was anyone but Jake who had ransacked our suite. He'd had enough time while we were locked in the conference room. Clearly, he was looking for something. The question was, what?

While Mickey was cleaning up and changing his clothes, Luis resumed his wandering around the room, and I picked up my stuff to repack it in my suitcase. This was a problem, because my suitcase was ruined. I found it sliced to shreds. I pulled out three dry-cleaning plastic bags from the closet. I shoved my clothes into them as I gathered them up from the floor, the furniture, the counter top, all the while taking inventory of what I was finding and trying to remember what I wasn't finding, straining to imagine anything at all that Jake would want to steal from me. That he would want to kidnap me for. I didn't have any fancy jewelry with me. I'm someone who pretty much wears the same jewelry all the time, so it's always on me: five rings, three bracelets, and a toe ring when I have sandals on.

I do like to change my earrings and usually travel with about ten pairs, even when I'm gone on two-day trips. I like choices.

But my earrings tend to be costume jewelry—not valuable. The extra pairs I had packed were all there, dumped out on the floor next to my jewelry case.

I also like interesting pins, and I had brought a stick pin with me to Chicago. I wear it in the lapel of a jacket, now and then I add it to a hat. It has a big fake pearl mounted on a blue enamel square. It was not with my earrings, it was not in my case. I wondered if I left it in Chicago, or if it was stolen. Maybe Jake couldn't tell a fake pearl from a real one.

I found my laptop tossed on the floor behind the couch. It didn't seem damaged. I turned it on and waited for it to boot up, checked the history of the document files—I keep only a few files on my laptop, just those I need with me when traveling—and noticed that each one of them had been opened the previous afternoon. This was an "Aha!" moment. Files. Jake wanted information I had, or thought I had.

I started mentally going through my current projects at work, all of the books I was promoting for the current season. *Take It Easy: A Thinking Man's Approach to Life; What, Me Worry?: A Pictorial History of* Mad Magazine; *My Father, Who Aren't in Heaven, Harold Be Thy Name: The Irrelevance of Religion in Post-Vietnam America;* and *The End of* Law and Order: *How One Show Changed Television Forever.* I couldn't see how any of these would encourage the wrath of thugs, mobsters, old women, or Las Vegas police. In fact, I doubted that much reading went on at all in Las Vegas, what with everyone gambling. Whatever books were available here probably amounted to fifty percent John Grisham and Sue Grafton, forty-five percent romance novels, and the balance, how to's and cookbooks. Okay, so maybe the *Mad Magazine* book would find an audience here, but why would anyone hold anything against Alfred E. Newman?

I shut down my laptop. Mickey was out of the bathroom, in clean clothes, going about the same business of gathering his belongings. He was checking his computer, too. We looked at each other and he shook his head. "He opened my files, but I don't know what he was looking for."

"Me neither," I said, "unless he collects unusual pins."

"What?"

"I'm missing a pin from my jewelry case. But it's not valuable. I probably left it in Chicago."

Mickey turned back to his laptop. Luis was still wandering around the room, examining everything like a cop would. He'd squat now and then, pace some more, then look up toward the ceiling at god knows what.

"Cassie," I suddenly said aloud. Luis and Mickey looked at me, waiting for more. "Cassie, my friend. She's staying at my apartment, housesitting Bonkers, my cat. I should call her, tell her I'm coming home today." They nodded and continued with what they were doing.

I got an outside line on the hotel phone and dialed my home number. It rang twice, then I heard a man's voice answer, "Hello?" My heart jumped. I was unnerved.

"Who is this?" I asked. Mickey and Luis stopped what they were doing, picking up on my weird voice.

"You've reached the Starkey residence. Who's calling, please?"

"Who are you and why are you in my apartment?" I wasn't yelling. I was quiet. I was getting used to being scared, and I got scared a lot sooner than perhaps I would have on any other day.

"This is Beatrice Starkey?"

"Yes, yes, it is, where is Cassie?"

A pause. Oh, the worst pause of my life.

"Where are you, Ms. Starkey?"

"Where is Cassie? What is going on?"

Another pause. Some voices in the background.

"Ms. Starkey, this is Sergeant Franklin, SFPD. I'm sorry to tell you, Cassie Hobbs is dead. It appears she was murdered."

That's when I yelled something unintelligible, some animal scream buried deep inside me. Mickey leaped over the coffee table in time to catch me before I fell to the floor.

Chapter Nine

I was lying on the floor, my head in Mickey's lap, his face close to mine, his voice repeating my name, and I grabbed onto him for all my life. He drew me up to sit and he held me and rocked me while I cried all over his t-shirt. Luis was on the phone, talking to Sergeant Franklin in a low voice. I couldn't hear what he was saying. I pushed away from Mickey suddenly and whispered, "Bonkers, my cat. Is my cat okay?"

Mickey turned toward Luis. "Ask about Annabelle's cat. Is it there? Is it okay?"

Luis kept speaking into the phone, then took the receiver away from his face. "The cat is fine. Hiding under the bed. But not harmed." I went back to my position in Mickey's arms and eventually stopped crying.

Luis hung up the phone, walked over and sat down on a chair facing us. "Do you want to hear this now?" I nodded. "Someone broke into your apartment Sunday night. The lock was smashed."

"But I have two dead bolts."

"Well, either Cassie didn't lock them, or the perp somehow busted them. The police think that no one was home at the time, and then Cassie unfortunately showed up when the murderer was there. She surprised him. He hit her head with something, and that's what killed her."

"Do they know it was only one guy, not more than that?" Mickey asked.

"So far, that's what they think. They don't have the murder weapon yet. They're dusting the apartment for prints. They've called Cassie's mother in Philadelphia. She's on her way to San Francisco." This piece of information started me weeping again. "The police said they knew you were in Las Vegas, but hadn't been able to reach you."

Mickey kissed the top of my head. "Annabelle, how did they know that?"

It took me a minute to remember. "I left a message for Cassie on my home phone. Sunday night. Said I was coming here with you but didn't give her any details, other than I'd be home a couple of days later than I originally planned."

"The police heard your message. Said it came in at 10:05 p.m. Also said it had already been picked up."

Mickey started. "Wait a minute. Annabelle leaves the message at 10:05, Cassie isn't there, Cassie comes home...when?"

"They figure around midnight."

"And she's attacked basically immediately?"

"It looks that way."

I shivered. "Whoever killed Cassie heard that message and found out where I was."

"Sunday night. And we got here Monday afternoon."

"And that's when Jake showed up."

"You mentioned my name in the message?"

I closed my eyes. "Yes. He must have checked all the hotels... found us here."

I stood up and went to the bathroom to wash my face. Whatever was going on had started with me, in California, and met up with us here in Las Vegas. In the meantime, it got my friend killed. What the hell was so important that someone was hot to get me, or get at me?

I walked back into the suite's living room. "Luis, what else? Was my apartment torn up? Things taken?"

"They won't know what might have been taken, but, yes, your apartment is a mess. They want you to come home and go through the place with them, answer questions, all that."

"Yeah. Of course. Okay. I'd better get out to the airport."

Mickey stood up. *"We'd* better get out to the airport. I'm coming with you."

I started weeping again. Luis hugged me while Mickey started gathering up all our stuff. "We need to buy a couple of suitcases downstairs."

"Don't go downstairs, Mickey," I sobbed.

"Don't worry. I'll call down and have them brought up." He picked up the phone.

A few minutes later the doorbell rang. Mickey opened the door, and a bellman stood there with two new suitcases, probably charged to Mickey's AmEx. Mickey tipped him, closed the door, then tossed the dry cleaning bags in the suitcases and started gathering up the rest of our things. I got control of my breathing and tears, gave Luis a weak smile, and helped Mickey finish the packing. We were ready to go. Luis said he would take us to the airport.

"What about all this damage to the room? What about Jake? Shouldn't we call the police before we leave?" I looked at Luis.

"I spoke with my partner. I gave him the basics, said there was a break-in here, but that because of a personal emergency you can't stick around. He's going to meet me here later. Mickey has the suite booked until tomorrow, so we'll sort this out with the hotel."

Mickey handed me my purse. "What's your home phone number, or any phone number? Luis needs to reach us, and Jake took our cell phones."

I recited it while Luis jotted it down. Then he gave us his card with his home and cell numbers. "I'll keep checking things out here. We should keep in touch, plan on talking to each other once a day. I recommend that you tell the SFPD everything that has gone on here, and in the meantime, I'll see what my partner and I can turn up." He paused. "Remember, please: Chuck Lowery, Jake, is a Vegas man. His power and his contacts don't extend beyond this city, as far as I know. But if all of this is related, and it is too coincidental not to be, then he's also a man for hire.

The connection is what's missing. The SF-Vegas connection."
He shook his head. "Well, no, amiga, you're the connection."
"Yup. Luis. I know. I just don't know why. Please believe me."
"I do."

"Let's go," said Mickey, and we grabbed our bags, headed
for the elevators, down to the street, and, once again, into Luis'
cab. We didn't see Jake or anyone else who looked familiar to
us in the casino. We didn't see Mary on the way. The airport
ride this time was uneventful. Mickey and I sat in the back seat,
holding hands. Every now and then he would squeeze mine,
and I would squeeze back, but we were each looking out our
respective windows.

Luis parked at the United curb, got out of the cab, and gave
me a hug. He held out his hand to shake Mickey's. Mickey took
it but then drew him close and gave him a man hug. "Thank
you." He pressed some cash into his hand.

"Not necessary, Mick."

"I insist, Luis. Fair is fair."

Luis pointed at Mickey with two fingers, like a gunslinger.
"I will call you tonight or tomorrow, or you call me any time."

We picked up our bags and started walking.

"Amigos!" Luis shouted. We turned around. "Thank you."

I walked a bit toward him. "For what, for chrissakes, Luis?"

"I'm back on track. You did that." Luis smiled at me, got in
his cab, and pulled away. I stood watching him until Mickey
called me, and I turned to head into the airport with him.

We were in time to make the flight I had booked in Chicago.
"You thought we would only be in Las Vegas for one night,
hmm?" Mickey gave my cap a playful tug and bought himself
a ticket. We sat toward the back, me in the middle, him on the
aisle, and a girl of about nineteen at the window, who listened
to her iPod the whole trip. Somehow I slept, my head resting
against Mickey's shoulder.

We landed at SFO, where Mickey rented a red Mustang
convertible. I chuckled. "Are you still trying to impress me?"

He winked at me. "Always."

Our flashy, look-at-us car headed north to San Francisco, the city I had always loved, the city where I thought I would always belong. But this homecoming felt dark and the streets, strange. The fog was cutting, not soothing. For the first time in my life, I didn't want to be there.

Chapter Ten

My apartment building is on the corner of Geary Boulevard and 23rd Avenue. I live on the second floor, right above a mom-and-pop bakery owned by an Italian couple. The luscious scents of freshly baked profiteroles, cannoli, and other sugary confections wake me each morning. The periodic roar of the Geary buses pulling in and out of the bus stop beneath my living-room window drove me crazy when I first moved in. It would completely drown out my TV or music. But I eventually got used to it. City noise has been a small price to pay for living by the ocean in a light-filled city that has embraced beatniks, hippies, and out-of-the-closet homosexuals. The rent, of course, is another matter. I can't really afford my apartment, and I've got way too much debt on my MasterCard. Retirement savings are a long way off.

Money doesn't interest me much. Expensive things aren't a necessity. Good taste and an eye for the great bargain keep my wardrobe up-to-date. Too many shoes, probably, but no Jimmy Choos or Manolos. Sales at Scandinavian Designs have furnished my apartment, so clean wood and simple lines offer uncluttered sanctuary in my four-room abode: bedroom, big living room, kitchen, and bathroom. I painted most of my walls what I call "clay-gray-green," the cool color that I plastered all over my face once when I thought I should be worrying about wrinkles and bought an expensive French clay mask. My kitchen is sunny with yellow tile counters, a red linoleum floor, and sunflower wallpaper I put up myself. It's a little over the top, but the room lands me smack dab in the middle of *Under the Tuscan Sun*. The movie bored me to tears, frankly, but the sunflowers that led Diane Lane to love and happiness have stuck with me.

If you've ever been to San Francisco, you know what a problem parking is. I don't own a car. I rent one when I need to get out of the city. Mickey drove around and around the avenues, from 20th up to 26th, and from Balboa to Lake, until we finally found a spot on 23rd and Anza, a block from my apartment. We got out of the car and shut the doors. Mickey grabbed his suitcase from the back seat.

"What are you doing? Don't you want to put the top up and lock it? We can leave our suitcases here."

"Nah. It's a convertible. If someone wants to steal it and the top is up, it's easy enough to slice through it with a good knife and get in. This way, we're saving the car some damage." He grabbed my suitcase, too, unlocked the trunk, and tossed them both in.

"Your logic escapes me." We were walking along the sidewalk now. "You've driven lots of convertibles, and this is how you came up with this theory?" We got to the front door to my building. I pulled my keys out of my purse.

Mickey smiled. "Not exactly. I used to steal cars. Convertibles were easy."

I jerked to look at him, dropping my keys. "Are you kidding me?"

That easy smile again. "High school. Long time ago." He picked up the keys and handed them to me. "Don't worry."

What, me worry? Even though I just found out I slept with a car thief who is now escorting me to a murder scene? I stuck the key in the lock, turned it, and pushed. We walked in and headed upstairs to my apartment. The creak of the old wooden stairs was louder than I remembered. The cream-colored walls, dingier.

My door was slightly ajar, and yellow crime-scene tape crisscrossed in front of it. It matched the tile in my kitchen. That's when I started to gulp for air, seeing how the edge of the door was bashed in, the locks were all busted up, and the figure of a uniformed policeman stood inside my hallway.

Mickey put his left arm around my shoulders and held tight. "Slow down, even breaths, slowly, you're okay." He lifted up the yellow tape.

The cop was about to speak when I said, "Hi, I live here." I immediately looked at his shoes to see if I could figure out what Luis meant, about cops wearing a certain kind of shoes. These looked sturdy and black, with laces.

"Ms. Starkey? Can I see some I.D.?"

"Okay. Can I see your badge?"

"It's right here on my chest, Miss. I'm Officer Wilson."

I was slightly embarrassed about that, but my only experience in situations like this came from TV, mostly *Law and Order* in all of its incarnations. I checked out his badge and then lifted my driver's license from my purse. After he examined it, Wilson nodded at Mickey, who took the hint and pulled out his license as well. Wilson examined it and handed it back to him before addressing me.

"Sergeant Franklin isn't here right now, but he asked me to tell you that he'll be back about six and wants you to wait here." I nodded. "He said to apologize for not meeting you at the airport, this being a murder case, but thought it would be best to see you here, since you are the primary..."

"Suspect?" Mickey interrupted. "Is that what you were going to say, officer? Because Annabelle wasn't even here Sunday night! She doesn't need this stress on top of everything else she's going through."

"Actually, no, Mr. Paxton, that's not what I was going to say." Wilson took a step toward Mickey. Mickey held his ground. Wilson's words were clipped. "I was going to say 'primary resident.'" He crossed his arms.

Mickey held up his hands, like he was imitating a goalpost. "Officer Wilson, we're a bit on edge, as you can probably imagine. We'll just take a seat and try to calm down."

"Sure thing, Mr. Paxton." He stepped aside as Mickey and I walked into the living room.

Sitting down was not easy. My home was a replay of the Las Vegas suite, with furniture turned upside down, books in heaps, shelves askew, a knife slice through the padding of the couch. I peered into my bedroom, looking for Bonkers, and saw the same mess. On my knees next to my bed, I lifted up the spread to see Bonkers' little black-and-white face peering at me as he crouched on all fours.

"Honey bun! C'mere!" I held out my hand, but he wasn't budging. I got up to get him some water, heading back to the kitchen through the living room and into the entrance alcove. That's when I saw the blood on the floor by the telephone table, gasped, moaned, and fled to the bathroom, where I heaved into the toilet.

Mickey came to the bathroom door but didn't watch me, just stood next to it. "It'll be okay, Annabelle." But he didn't sound okay, and I was throwing up, and Cassie's blood was on my floor.

He moved back into the living room. I eventually stood up, took off my glasses, washed my face, and rinsed out my mouth. I took my extra contact lenses out of the medicine cabinet and put them in. Then I sank down on the closed toilet seat, afraid to leave, unable to bear seeing the blood again. Mickey was on the phone.

"Luis?…Yeah, we're here.…Yes. The place is a mess.…No, he's not here right now, we're waiting for him. Any news there?… Mmm. Okay. There's still blood on the floor.…Yes, there's an officer here, but…Okay. Yeah. I'll ask him.…Yeah, after we see Franklin. Later…Yeah…Thanks." He hung up. "Officer?"

"Right here."

"May I have your permission to clean up this blood? Has forensics finished their work here?"

"I'm not sure, but I don't think so. We should wait for Sergeant Franklin before we touch that."

"No, sorry, no can do. Annabelle cannot see this blood again, do you understand? She can't. We have to clean it up."

"Well, look, I can't just…"

"You can call someone, right? You can call and find out if that would be okay?"

Wilson sighed. He was probably crossing his arms again. Then Mickey walked closer to him. "Wilson." He used a very measured voice. "You can call someone."

Wilson talked on his walkie-talkie, and Mickey came back to the bathroom. "You stay right there, Annabelle. I'll take care of this."

I couldn't open my eyes to thank him, but I waved my hand. Never had a man looked after me so well, ever, in my life. Let alone a car thief. Why was he so caring? Given my track record, how could I bet on any guy liking me enough to listen to me hurl without hurling himself—right out the door.

Wilson's voice faded away, so he must have stepped out into the hallway to have his conversation. Mickey waited by the bathroom door, as if guarding it, not letting anyone in and making sure I stayed put. Then Wilson called out. "It's okay. You can clean it up."

"Good. Thank you."

I should help clean up that blood. Why should Mickey have to do it? Still, my body wouldn't move. He rummaged around in the kitchen and found my Ajax and that big sponge I use for wiping down the kitchen walls after I have steamed them up but good from boiling more pasta than I need to eat. I plugged my ears, elbows on knees, kept my eyes shut, and tried to pretend I was sitting on the toilet on a cruise ship in the middle of the Caribbean. That was hopeless. Instead my mind retraced my walk up the apartment stairs to my front door, and came up with a lot of questions.

"Annabelle?" I opened my eyes and removed my fingers. Mickey squatted down in front of me and took one hand in his. Nice of him not to notice the bit of earwax on its tip. "I'm sorry. Most of the blood is gone, but there's a stain. I can't get that up."

I squeezed his hand. "Okay. Thanks."

"But I found a small braided rug in the corner of your bedroom, and I put that over it."

I drew him to me then, my arms around his neck, pressing the side of my face against his. "What's your middle name?"

"Thomas."

"Thank you, Michael Thomas Paxton."

"Sure."

We both stood up and walked into the living room, taking our time looking around at the mayhem. And that's when Sergeant Franklin walked in.

"Wilson?"

"Sir."

"They're here?"

"Yes, sir."

We turned around to meet Franklin. It's true I was not in a trusting mood, and it's true that I was imagining conspiracies behind every handshake, but it got far too weird when Mickey saw Franklin and said, "Brad? Brad Franklin? Is that really you? Jesus!" before holding out his hand.

Brad Franklin used his hand to pull Mickey into a bear hug. "Surprise, surprise, Paxton! I knew it was you when I talked to the Las Vegas detective, Luis Maldonado. How's everything going in New York? Man, how long has it been?"

"Christ, probably twelve years. Damn." Mickey acted nonplussed. "A cop? You're a cop? When did that happen? The last time I saw you, you were trying to sell futures for a brokerage house."

"Well, that got old quick, and I thought, what the hell, I'll see if I can get a real job. Signed up, in fact, soon after I last saw you. I guess you inspired…"

Mickey jumped in. "Patty? How's Patty?" Franklin kept gripping Mickey's hand in a shake and pumping their arms up and down during this exchange. Mickey was trying to pull away. I just gawked.

"Ah, well, didn't work. We got divorced about five years ago. The police world didn't suit her, you might say."

"Hmmm. Yeah." They finally let go of each other.

"What about you? What was her name, um…Laurie?"

Okay, now I was annoyed. I guess I coughed or shuffled my feet, and the two long-lost pals swiftly shifted their loving gazes from each other to me. Franklin spoke first.

"I'm so sorry, Ms. Starkey. You must be Beatrice Starkey. I'm Brad Franklin. Sorry about all of this." He held out his hand and I shook it.

"Thanks. So you guys…?"

Mickey put his arm around my shoulders. "Annabelle, Brad and I were in college together at Amherst. I majored in English and Brad…what *did* you major in, Brad? Frisbee?" Franklin snorted.

"We'll catch up later, Mick." He winked at his old pal, then shifted his expression and turned to me again. "Right now we have to talk about your friend Cassie and what happened here Sunday night."

"Okay. I'll start. I have a lot of questions." I held his gaze.

Franklin paused and I saw his mouth twitch slightly. "Okay, shoot." Then he stuck his hands in his pockets, moved his legs a bit wider apart than his hips, locked his knees, and waited.

"How come we weren't met at the airport, seeing as how this is a murder case, and all?"

Brad laughed. "Well, usually we don't worry about one of…"

Mickey interrupted him again. "Brad just said, he remembers me from the old days."

Brad paused to study Mickey for a few seconds. Whatever passed between them was creepy.

"Sounds pretty casual to me. You haven't seen Mickey in ten years. How do you know he's not some criminal? I mean, he used to steal cars." Mickey let his arm drop and gave me a look that I read as, "What has gotten into you, little lady?" which got me even more riled up.

Franklin held his position a moment, moving his eyes back and forth before relaxing into a pleasant smile. "Mick isn't a criminal, I know that. But you got me on the other thing."

"What?"

"You're right. It would have been sloppy police work not to meet you at the airport. But someone did. Followed you here. If you were going to take off somewhere, we wanted to know where you'd go."

Mickey shrugged at my glare. "We weren't really paying attention to people or cars around us."

"Hey, we're good at what we do. You wouldn't have seen my guy anyway." He fiddled with coins in his pocket. "Do you have another question?"

"Yeah. My next one is, if the locks on the door were broken when Cassie got back here, why would she have come into the apartment?"

Franklin was sizing me up. "She didn't. It looks like the intruder grabbed her right when she reached the top of the stairs and pulled her into your apartment. He was in the hallway waiting for her. He may have been ready to leave and seen or heard her come in the front door of the building. We found her purse out in the hallway, like she dropped it there."

Mickey said, "But he hit her in the alcove of the apartment."

"Yes, he got her inside and then hit her over the head."

"With what?" I asked.

"We don't have a murder weapon yet. But it could have been any number of things, heavy and hard. His gun, if he had one."

"Any prints yet?"

He rolled his eyes, like that was the dumbest question he'd ever heard. "Well, sure, we found a lot of prints. But if this guy was careful, they'll all be yours and Cassie's, and any other friends' you may have had in your apartment." Franklin motioned to my sliced-up sofa. "Shall we sit down now and talk about you?"

"Okay, but first I've got to get water for my cat." I tiptoed through the kitchen, stepping around, over, and right on top of forks, knives, spoons, and broken coffee mugs. Bonkers' food and water dishes were on the floor next to the refrigerator. I picked them both up and rinsed them out, put some kibble in one and some water in the other, and gingerly made my way back to the bedroom. Kneeling down, I pushed the two dishes underneath the bed and peeked at Bonkers. He hadn't moved.

"Sugar pie, here's some yummy food and some water. I want you to eat." I held out my hand again. Bonkers stayed put, eyes wild. I waited for a minute, my hand outstretched, and then gave up.

I could hear the two men speaking quietly. They stopped abruptly when I came in and sat down on the sofa next to Mickey. Franklin had righted my butterfly chair and was sitting in it, looking silly. Were policemen supposed to look so comfortable? And why was Mickey looking so *un*comfortable?

"I'm starving," I suddenly announced. We hadn't eaten anything except airplane crackers since breakfast.

Mickey took my hand. "Brad, can we go somewhere and talk about all of this over dinner?"

"There's a good little Italian place on Clement, a short walk." I stood up. "Really, I need to eat."

Franklin tilted his head to the side as if he were studying something on the wall and then turned back. "Okay. Not the usual procedure, but I don't see any harm in it." He and Mickey stood up and I picked up my purse.

When they headed for the door, I checked Bonkers one more time. He was lapping up some water. "Good kitty." I reached under to pet him, and he let me. Then I saw it. The little notepad I keep on my bedside table. Bonkers had been crouching on it. I reached for it and was about to toss it onto the table when I noticed that part of the last page torn off was still attached. Now, I'm not a neat freak or anything, but I would never leave a torn bit like that attached to a notepad. Someone had used this. I could feel indentations on the top full page. I fumbled around in the table drawer—which is definitely *not* the drawer of a neat freak—until I found a pencil. I felt like Nancy Drew, rubbing the pencil over the top sheet. Sure enough, a message emerged—"Georgia Browning" and a phone number.

I had never heard of Georgia Browning. How had the police missed the notepad? Maybe Bonkers had been sitting on it under the bed, and Bonkers can be ferocious when he senses danger. They probably let him be. But how did this end up under my bed in the first place? And who was Georgia Browning?

I took a quick breath and was about to call out to Mickey, but instead I stuck the notepad in my back pocket without a word. I figured Cassie had written the message on the pad—she had been staying in my apartment for several days, after all—and maybe Georgia was her friend. I'd find out who Georgia was before saying anything to the police, and especially to Brad. I didn't like the way he stared at me when he talked, like he thought I was either guilty or stupid.

I joined the guys waiting at my front door. "Bonkers still seems really afraid. It makes me wonder how much he saw, or understood, or, well, experienced, however cats experience things."

Franklin let out a sharp guffaw at that, and it wasn't empathetic in the least. It bordered on nasty. "That cat of yours is one mean feline—took a swipe at me and tried to bite me when I reached for it, the little pisser." In that moment, I hated him.

Mickey took my hand and squeezed it. "The good news is he's safe."

I pulled my long black sweater off the hook in the hallway, put it on, and half-smiled at the two men. Officer Wilson stayed behind as the three of us walked down the stairs to dinner.

Chapter Eleven

Mickey and I stayed at the Sheraton Palace that night, downtown. It's my favorite San Francisco hotel. The rooms are spacious and furnished with warm, cozy furniture and beds so comfortable you wish you could contract some prolonged, painless, nonfatal, contagious disease which would give you no choice but to stay bedridden for at least thirty days. With, of course, the man you were falling in love with, who had also contracted the same benign but debilitating ailment. And, with an unlimited room service budget. Oh—and sexy pajamas. For yourself and him.

Sergeant Franklin had spent a couple of hours with us at dinner, asking me about the history of my relationship with Cassie for the first hour, and then jogging down memory lane with Mickey about college and sports and women and family. It wasn't clear to me why they had been out of touch for so long, but these things happen. Time gets away from people, and before you know it, a couple of weeks have turned into a couple of years.

I found out that Laurie was Mickey's girlfriend in college and, I surmised, for a few years following. She was a highly motivated law student who currently was working for a high-profile firm specializing in corporate law, which I took to mean mergers, acquisitions, hostile takeovers, and big, big bucks. Mickey's explanation for their break-up was brief: "Politics. Hers offended mine; mine offended hers. It turned out that we didn't love each other enough to put up with all that. She probably voted for Dubya."

Brad's questions to me were all about how well I knew Cassie. I explained that I knew her pretty well, but our friendship was defined by and limited to our sporadic weekend jaunts. We had been spending Saturday mornings together—whenever other plans didn't get in the way—at a ninety-minute yoga class, followed by a brief breakfast at the café next to the yoga studio, and then an hour-long hike wherever we decided to go.

He interrupted at one point. "Lovers? Did she have a lot of them, or was she a one-man kind of girl?"

His not-so-subtle sneer made me want to spit at him. I hated him all over again. But I gulped Chianti instead.

"She's been seeing someone recently, a lawyer, but I don't know who it was."

Recently, my hikes with Cassie had become easy walks through Golden Gate Park or had been abandoned altogether, since Cassie was hot to spend as much time as she could with her new squeeze on the weekends.

Brad tore off a piece of garlic bread. "Tell me more."

I reached for my Chianti again, but the glass was empty. Mickey poured me another.

Cassie worked for Whole Foods, managing their produce department. She was a healthy-food-and-exercise proponent, but she believed in enjoying life in the here and now. She was the only yogini I knew who smoked Camels. I also knew she was an only child and her father had died a couple of years ago. She had grown up in a suburb of Philadelphia, where her mother still lived. They were close. I asked Brad where Cassie's mother was—had she arrived in San Francisco?

"Yes, she has been to the station to identify the body, and she's staying with friends in Pacific Heights. Do you know Mrs. Hobbs?"

"No, I've never met her."

"Well, she told me that she is planning on having a service out here for Cassie's friends, and then another one back east. She also mentioned that she would like to see you."

I brought my hand to my forehead. "Oh, god. Really? I wouldn't want to see me. Her only daughter was murdered in my apartment…" I took another swallow of wine.

Mickey patted my knee. "You were Cassie's friend. Mrs. Hobbs knows that." I grabbed his hand. We worked it out that Brad would give Cassie's mother the number at the hotel, so that she could call when she was ready. Brad said the SFPD would have a patrol unit at my apartment for at least another day, in case whoever killed Cassie came back for me. I guess that had occurred to me already, but hearing him say it so matter-of-factly made me feel like my chair had been jerked out from under me.

Mickey squeezed my hand, then suggested that we buy new cell phones first thing in the morning and repair the lock on my apartment, seeing as how my landlord was in Costa Rica on vacation.

"Sounds like a plan." I took a last swig of Chianti.

When we left the restaurant and walked back to our respective vehicles, Mickey and Brad gave each other a quick high-five, and Brad shook my hand. "I'll be in touch with you tomorrow. Get some sleep. And let me know tomorrow if you discover anything of value missing from your apartment."

"Okay, but I don't have valuable stuff." We started walking away from each other, and then I channeled Peter Falk as Columbo, because I turned around and called after Brad. "Were there any other messages on my answering machine, besides the one I left for Cassie on Sunday night?"

He stopped and turned to me, looked off down the street, and then back at me. "No. Just that one." He gave us a little wave, then continued on his way.

I turned and took Mickey's arm. Georgia Browning. Did Cassie write her name down because Georgia had called me?

We got in the Mustang and drove downtown to the hotel. After we got to our room, I closed and locked the door, fell onto the bed, and studied the ceiling. Mickey went into the bathroom, and soon I was sound asleep.

◇◇◇

When I woke up the next morning, I was naked and under the covers. Mickey was already up, wearing a white hotel bathrobe, sitting at the small desk. He had his laptop plugged in and was typing away on it, now and then sipping from a cup of coffee. I noticed a tray with a silver pot and two cups on it, cream and sugar.

"Hey," I said.

"Hey." He swiveled in his chair and winked at me. He looked tired.

"Room service brought that and I didn't even hear them?"

"You've been out cold." He poured coffee in the second cup and brought it over to me, while I scooted myself into a sitting position. He sat down on the edge of the bed and gave me a kiss. "Morning."

I smiled and took a swallow of coffee. "Mmmm." Then I put the cup and saucer down on the bedside table. "What time is it?"

"Ten o'clock."

"What? I slept for twelve hours?"

"Yes, indeed, you did. You needed to."

I scanned the room again and saw my clothes neatly stacked on the easy chair, by the window. "Looks like you took good care of me, once again."

"My pleasure." Mickey smiled and then stood up. "We have a busy day."

"Yup, I should get up and take a shower. We've got to get the lock, and the cell phones. We should drive up to Santa Rosa. We should call Luis, and…"

"Who's Georgia Browning?"

I froze. Mickey just stood there. "Any time, Annabelle."

"I'm sorry. I was going to tell you about her last night, but I passed out." I think this was true.

He tilted his head slightly and narrowed his eyes. "Well, you can tell me about her now. I found the notepad in your pocket when I undressed you last night. And, before you assume that I was rifling through your pockets"—he was right, I was about to accuse him of this—"let me say in my defense that as I was folding your pants I felt something in the pocket and simply pulled it out so that it wouldn't get lost, or bent, or whatever."

"Okay."

"So, who is she?"

"I don't know."

He picked up the notepad from the desk. "So why was this in your pocket?"

"I found it under my bed. Bonkers had been sitting on it."

"Your cat sits on notepads?"

"Clearly you're not a cat person. He likes paper. He curls up with it. Sometime try reading a newspaper with him around. Or a book. He likes to play with postcards."

"And you said nothing to Brad because…?"

I pulled the covers up closer to my neck. "Because I hate him and I don't trust him."

Mickey was skeptical. "Really? Wow. Kind of a snap judgment, don't you think?"

"I've been making a lot of those lately. I mean, here I am with you, and I just met you three days ago. Are you going to tell me that was a mistake?"

"Touché." He came back over to the bed and sat on the edge again. "So, what do you think this lawyer Georgia Browning has to do with anything?

I sat straight up with a start. "LAWYER? How do you know she's a lawyer?"

"I Googled her. She has an office on Chestnut Street."

"Maybe she's Cassie's lover!"

"What?"

"I didn't want Brad to come to any weirdo-psycho-lesbian conclusions about Cassie, so that's why I told him only that she was in love with a lawyer, not that the lawyer was a woman."

Mickey sighed. "Annabelle, you should tell Brad what you know and not leave out important details, like sexual orientation and notepads under cats!"

I closed my eyes. "Maybe."

"You think?" He paused. "Why would Cassie write her lover's name and phone number on a piece of paper that ended up under Bonkers?"

I looked at him. "I don't know. Maybe she was doodling one day…"

"Or maybe Georgia called you and doesn't even know Cassie."

"I thought of that, too. That's why I asked Brad if there were any other messages on my machine. Maybe Cassie wrote this as a phone message."

He waved the pad in the air. "But how did this end up on the floor?"

"I keep it on the table by the bed. She could have written the message and torn it off, and then knocked it on the floor."

"And done what with the message?"

I shook my head. "I don't know."

Mickey stood up. He walked over to the windows and opened the heavy drapes. Sunlight streamed in, making stripes on the navy blue carpet and illuminating his worried face. "I don't like this, Annabelle. I don't like to keep secrets from Brad, from the police."

I got up and retrieved the other terry bathrobe from the closet, put it on, and went to put my arm around Mickey's waist. "I don't trust anyone in all this mess, except you." As soon as I said that, my throat tightened and I had to swallow. After the weird way he was acting around Brad the night before, I reminded myself that I really didn't know Mickey very well. "But I especially don't trust Brad Franklin. He's got a nasty edge to him. Why should I trust a man anymore just because he's carrying a badge? I don't know who the bad guys are or the good guys. I don't like the coincidence of your old friend showing up on this scene. It's too weird. I know he's your friend, but that's how I feel."

Mickey put his arm around my shoulders. We both kept looking out the windows onto bustling Market Street, thronged with business people, panhandlers, and shoppers. A self-proclaimed soapbox preacher used a megaphone to warn of imminent doom. Mickey sighed. "It is weird. It's so weird that this morning I've been checking out Brad on the Internet." He drew me closer to him. "I wasn't sure I could trust him either. He's a creep."

"What do you mean? I thought you were long lost friends."

"Not really. Friends, sort of, for a while. He was a mean drunk."

"What did you find out online?"

"Everything he told us last night is true. He has been with the SFPD for about ten years, he got a divorce five years ago. He's definitely a sergeant."

"Well, that's good to know. But..."

"But so is Chuck Lowery a policeman, right?"

"Right." I turned toward Mickey. "Look, I *have* to go see Georgia. I owe it to Cassie, I owe it to you, to get some answers. We can fill Brad in later. If you don't want to come, I understand, but I'm going to see her, and, well, that's that, Paxton." I stood arms akimbo and felt like John Wayne. Only smaller.

Mickey took my hands. "Okay, *Starkey*. You take a shower, and I'll call the locksmith. We'll get that door taken care of first, then we'll go see Georgia Browning. But after we talk to her, we tell Brad about her."

"Unless we agree that there is a compelling reason not to."

It took Mickey a moment before he agreed. "Okay."

I put my arms around his neck and kissed him on the mouth. My bathrobe fell open, and his hands came to my waist and he pulled me to him. We hugged each other while he stroked my back. I undid the tie around his bathrobe, pulled it off of his shoulders, and let it fall to the floor. I wriggled out of mine, which landed in a lump at my feet. I led Mickey to the bed by the hand, and we both climbed in under the pillowy comforter and smooth sheet. When we got up next, it was almost noon.

Chapter Twelve

Mickey told me over breakfast, at a we-serve-eggs-all-day retro diner a few blocks from the hotel, that he had been taking care of office emails that morning, too, besides investigating his old friend. He wrote to his boss that some "personal difficulties" had come up, that he wasn't sure when he'd be back in the office, but that he would stay in touch by email and phone, and would make sure that all of the follow-ups necessary for meetings at the book convention were taken care of. Mickey had a full-time assistant at the office, and, as he put it, "He's Mr. Reliable, and after all of this is sorted out, he'll be Mr. Reliable with a Big Raise."

That struck me as odd. At my company, "Big Raise" was a phrase I'd never heard, especially for a publicity manager like me, let alone a sales assistant. But Mickey had mentioned something about them releasing a new blockbuster akin to J. K. Rowling's *Harry Potter,* so I guessed his company could be doing a lot better than mine.

I wasn't expected back until the next week. I was on vacation, to relax for a few days following the book convention. Hah.

We both had Sprint cell phone service, and there was a Sprint store on the way to my apartment, so we stopped to buy phones. We met the locksmith at three. He was already there when we arrived, and a uniformed policeman was with him. It took the locksmith only about thirty minutes to install a new deadbolt and a new handle with a lock, and new keys for both. The door was still a bit bashed in on its edge, but that would have to be dealt with later. We thanked the officer for his help, and I gave the locksmith a check.

After searching through my belongings, I didn't determine that anything was missing.

Bonkers was still under the bed. I changed his litter box and refilled his food and water dish, happy to see them both depleted.

We drove the Mustang, top down, to Georgia Browning's offices in the Marina district on Chestnut Street. After parking in a public garage, we walked a couple of blocks to an old, restored Victorian.

The receptionist greeted us. "Hello, can I help you?"

Mickey answered. "We're here to see Georgia Browning."

"Do you have an appointment?"

"No, actually…"

"Well, I'm sorry, but she doesn't see drop-ins. Would you like to schedule…"

"Look," I jumped in. "We're here on an urgent personal matter. It's very urgent, in fact. Could be a matter of life and death." I folded my arms.

Mickey cleared his throat. "It *is* important, if you'd be so kind as to let her know we're here."

She frowned, but I didn't flinch. She picked up the phone and punched in three numbers, explained that we were there and added, "It might be important." She hung up. "Georgia will see you. Please go upstairs and turn left at the top. Her office is right there."

Mickey thanked her, and we took the stairs.

When we walked in, Georgia Browning stood up, walked out from behind her desk, held out her hand, and said, "Ms. Starkey, Mr. Paxton, how can I help you?"

She was slight in build and about my height, around five foot seven. Her blond hair was in an updo, and it looked like she had a lot of it. She was dressed in a chic dark green wool suit, jacket and pants, and wore fashionable black spike high heels. Her small diamond earrings and long, gold necklace were perfect accessories to the suit. She was very professional, but she seemed nervous. After she shook our hands, she fidgeted with her necklace. We all sat down. I noticed a framed photograph on her desk of a man and two children. If Georgia was Cassie's lover, I guessed she was in the closet.

I smiled at her. "I found your name on a notepad in my apartment. Did you call me?"

Her face twitched the slightest bit, and her complexion paled. I had never seen that happen to anyone before, such a sudden loss of color.

She glanced from me to Mickey then back to me again. "Why, no, I didn't call you. I don't know you, do I?"

I shook my head. "No. Do you know Cassie Hobbs?"

She couldn't turn any whiter, but now she was twisting her necklace around her fingers like she was playing a game of Cat's Cradle. "No, no, I can't say that I do."

Mickey put his hand on my knee. "Ms. Browning, Cassie Hobbs was murdered in Annabelle's apartment Sunday night, and we found your name. That's why we're here. We thought you might have some information that could help us figure out what happened."

Georgia stood up. "Well, for heaven's sake, I know nothing about this. I've never heard of this person."

"Cassie," I said.

"Cassie, yes. I'm sorry, but I'm afraid I'm no help to you. Perhaps she was going to call me about a legal matter?"

I looked at Mickey. He nodded at Georgia. "Perhaps. But you haven't heard from her?"

Georgia shook her head.

"What kind of law do you practice?" I asked.

"Estates, wills, trusts, personal financial matters…" Her voice trailed off as she sat back down and pulled her appointment book in front of her. "Listen, I have a busy day and I'm afraid I'm out of time. I'm sorry I can't be more helpful." She put on her best attorney face and managed a tight-lipped smile.

I could see her appointment book from where I was sitting. There was nothing written on the open pages.

Mickey smiled back and stood. "We understand. Sorry to bother you. Thank you for your time." He tossed me a let's-get-out-of-here look.

Mickey and I split down the stairs, passing the receptionist on her way up, and continued to the front door. At least, I walked to the door, before I noticed Mickey wasn't with me. I turned around and saw him staring at the receptionist's desk.

"Mickey, what are you doing?" I joined him.

"Look at this." He picked up an eight-by-ten glossy color photograph that was lying on top of a manila envelope. A group of old people, all sitting together in a kind of living room, held a banner that read, "Thank you, Georgia!" Georgia occupied the center seat in the middle of the group, wearing a wide-brim hat. The old woman to her left was Nana, my grandmother. Mary Rosen was sitting to her right.

Mickey put the photo back on the desk, aimed his new phone and snapped a picture of the picture. Then he grabbed my arm and rushed me out the door.

Chapter Thirteen

"We've got to go see Brad right away." Mickey was embracing his inner racecar-driver self, channeling Mario Andretti or Jeff Gordon while he floored the Mustang. "Annabelle, I'm going to the police station."

I couldn't argue with him. I was simply stunned by that photo.

Mickey was talking as fast as Joe Pesci's Leo Getz character in the *Lethal Weapon* movies, which wasn't the least bit comforting, since Leo was not only annoying, he screwed things up. "Okay okay okay. We're going to tell Brad that we found Georgia, and she's the link between Cassie getting killed and what happened in Las Vegas, or something. Or that Mary Rosen really did have something to do with Jake, or Chuck, or whatever his name is."

I wanted to poke my head out of the side of the car like a dog, and have the wind blow my hair back, while I panted. Instead, I tried not to hyperventilate.

"I should call Luis. That's what I should do." Mickey reached for his cell phone and tried to start dialing while heading up Gough Street, and I do mean up. It's one of those classic steep San Francisco streets. But he swerved, nearly hit a tree, then dropped the phone. "Damn it!"

I picked it up. "I'll call him. You drive. What's the number?"

"Never mind. I'll do it later." He held out his hand for the phone.

But I scrolled down the "contacts" menu and saw Luis' number. "It's right here. I'll call him."

"I entered a few numbers while we were waiting for the locksmith to finish, but I'll call him when we stop. I want to talk to him." Mickey was wiggling his fingers at me, still wanting the phone.

"Don't drive with one hand. You're going to kill us." I hit the talk button. I heard the phone ring, and then "Yes, this is Luis." Mickey slapped his palm back on the steering wheel.

"Luis, hi, it's Annabelle."

"Amiga. Good to hear your voice. How are you? Where are you?"

"Mickey is driving like a madman right now to a San Francisco police station, and I'm calling you because we have uncovered some information. Where are you right now? Mickey, turn left at the next corner."

Luis was sitting in his captain's office at his precinct station, waiting to meet with him. "I'm staring at a photo, a black-and-white glossy of Captain Buddy Anderson receiving an award from the Las Vegas Chamber of Commerce for 'Excellence in Community Service.'"

"Ah. And did he deserve it?"

Mickey, who had turned onto Bush Street and was at that moment careening downhill with what looked like pure exhilaration, but what was probably all-out panic, yelled sharply, "Did who deserve what?" at the same time that Luis answered, "Actually, yes. He's a good man. Spends a lot of time with poor kids. Lost one of his own a few years back."

"It sounds like you respect him. Are you going to tell him about Jake? I mean, Chuck?"

"Who? Who does he respect? Who is he going to tell about Jake?" Mickey, following my wildly gesticulating hand, was turning a corner now onto Hyde, having made it through all of the green lights on Bush Street without stopping, and started honking his horn at some hapless pedestrian who hadn't been expecting the Batmobile to come roaring toward him.

"Mickey, will you chill? Please? Jeez. Luis, sorry, I couldn't hear you, Mickey is kind of crazed right now and, well, it's hard to explain."

"I said, yes, I am here to talk to him about Chuck, and in fact, I see him coming now, so I will have to call you back."

"Wait, Luis, just one thing. One name. Georgia Browning. We think she's in on this, whatever it is. She's a lawyer. She's connected to Tall Oaks and Mary Rosen. She might have been connected to Cassie or to her killer, we don't know. Or she might have killed Cassie. Or…"

"WHICH WAY?" cried Mickey. He made a sudden right onto Market Street, slammed his foot on the brake, and steered the Mustang over to a curb painted red. We were both flung forward in our seats, and when the car came to a complete stop, we were flung back again.

I glared at Mickey. "Will you calm down? You should have gone straight across Market." He reached for the phone but I kept it to my ear. "Sorry, Luis, didn't hear you again."

"I have to go now, Annabelle. I wrote the name down. I will call you later. Hasta luego." He hung up.

"Mickey, we can't park here, it's a red zone."

"Give me my phone."

"Fine. Here it is." I tossed it to him. He grabbed it out of the air and stuck it back in his sport coat pocket. "What did Luis say?"

"He couldn't talk, he was waiting to meet with his captain, to speak with him about Jake. I mean, Chuck. But he wrote Georgia's name down." Mickey was shaking his head and wagging his finger at me.

"What? Will you stop that?" I grabbed his finger.

He kept shaking his head. "I should have never gone along with this. We might have just met with Cassie's *murderer*…"

"Or her lover…"

"*Lover?* Did you not see the picture on her desk of her husband and kids?"

"Mickey, we can't park here."

"You already said that."

"I know. But we're still here."

"Annabelle, Georgia was not Cassie's lover."

"You don't know that. She might have been in the closet."

"So, you think she *was* Cassie's lover, and she just happened to have done some sort of charity work or something for Tall Oaks, and that's some big coincidence?"

"I don't know, probably not. But Georgia was so nervous, she knew something, something big. So the first two things I think of are, one, she was Cassie's lover, or two, she killed her."

"Okay, maybe she did know Cassie. Maybe she was getting close to Cassie to try to get close to you." Mickey ran his hands through his hair. "But then why would she kill Cassie?"

"Maybe Cassie found out about something Georgia was up to." I paused. "But Mickey, we really don't know that Georgia was up to anything. They may have been lovers, and it could be a coincidence that Georgia did some legal work for Tall Oaks."

"I don't believe in coincidence."

"It's not something to believe in, Mickey. It's not like a religion or something. Happenstance, circumstance, things happen. Like, you and me. We just happened to meet in Chicago."

"What coincidence is there in that?"

"I don't know, okay? I don't know!" Right then I felt a little electric buzz against my butt. "What's wrong with this car?"

"What do you mean?"

"I'm getting electrocuted, or laser beamed, or…" I reached to my back pocket and felt my new phone there. I had it on "vibrator" mode. I pulled it out and flipped it open. "Hello?"

"Is this Annabelle?" A woman's voice.

"Yes," I answered warily. "Who is this please?" Mickey fiddled with his phone.

"Annabelle, dear, this is Beth Hobbs. Cassie's mother."

"Oh! Mrs. Hobbs!" Mickey relaxed back in his seat and dropped his head against the headrest. The hotel phone system allowed you to leave an answering message on your room phone. I had left one giving my new cell phone number. "I'm so glad you called me. Are you all right? Well, no, of course you're not. You must be…oh jeez, um, the police told me you are with friends, and I hope that's right. I am glad you called. I…"

"I *am* with friends, and I wanted to see if we could get together, perhaps tomorrow, and I also wanted to know if you have spoken to Kirsten."

"Kirsten?"

"Yes, Cassie's friend, Kirsten."

"I'm sorry, I don't know who that is."

Beth Hobbs was silent for what felt like a full minute. "Annabelle, did you know that my daughter was gay?"

I started to feel queasy. I bent over my knees. I answered her in a quiet voice. "Yes, I did know. I didn't know that you knew."

"She just told me…" Beth's voice cracked and she stopped. "She just told me a few days ago. She called to tell me that she had fallen in love, and that she didn't want to keep it a secret from me, and that she had fallen in love with a woman."

I closed my eyes, my head was between my knees. "I see. And, Mrs. Hobbs, I guess she told you that this woman's name was Kirsten?"

I knew the answer before she spoke, and the inside of my head was swimming. "Yes, and I haven't reached her yet."

I took a deep breath. "I'm so sorry, Mrs. Hobbs. Cassie told me she was falling for someone, but she didn't tell me much about her. She told me she didn't want to give me any details until she was sure about the relationship. I didn't even know her name was Kirsten."

At that, I felt Mickey sit up to my left.

"That's all right." Her voice cracked, and I heard her take a deep breath. "If you'd like to get together tomorrow sometime, I'd like to meet you."

I sat up and focused on the fire hydrant to our right. "Sure. I have to drive up to Santa Rosa, but how about breakfast, or coffee in the morning?" We agreed to meet for coffee at ten at Café Eduardo on Bush Street at Powell, and said goodbye.

Mickey was watching me. He had calmed down, his eyes had gone soft. He reached over and put his hand on my shoulder, comforting me. Back to being kind and looking after me. I wondered if he was like that with everyone, or if I had truly managed to sweep him off his feet. I shook that thought out of my head. No sense in imagining he was my Mr. Darcy and I was his Elizabeth Bennet in some modern-day version of *Pride and Prejudice.* Mickey would find me too proud and headstrong for him. I would discover he was prejudiced against women with oversized ears and a big mouth. I had never bewitched a man, body and soul, like Keira Knightly did. That long neck of hers probably helped.

"Mickey, we can't park here."

"I'm moving." He squeezed my shoulder before he turned the key in the ignition and headed up Market Street, driving the speed limit and stopping courteously for pedestrians.

Chapter Fourteen

The police station was bustling, pretty close to five when we walked in the front door. Mickey told the uniformed woman behind the desk that we were there to see Brad, and she indicated where we should sit while she found him for us. While we waited, I casually looked around for Michael Douglas and Karl Malden, having recently seen some reruns of *The Streets of San Francisco* on late-night television. Anything to help me stop thinking about meeting with Brad the Bad Franklin.

I saw the ladies room down the hall and told Mickey I'd be right back. On my way I passed Franklin sitting at a desk in an office to my right. He was gesticulating and practically spitting his words into his cell phone. I managed to squeeze up next to the open door, where he couldn't see me, so that I could hear him.

"We're running out of time. I've had it with the chief. He's all over my ass, all of that shit about 'proper investigation technique.' I'd like to see him try to get a confession without a little muscle." Pause. "Take it easy. We'll be long gone before he can…" Pause. "Yeah. Later." He hung up.

I skedaddled into the bathroom and a few minutes later returned to my seat next to Mickey. He rested his arm on my thigh and closed his hand lightly over my knee. I crossed my arms over my chest, trying to keep any internal combustion from exploding through my sternum.

Brad walked up to us a few minutes later. "You both look worn out. Everything okay?"

"No, not really." Mickey grimaced.

"C'mon. Let's go talk in the room at the end of the hall." Brad pointed at a wall of vending machines behind us. "Either of you want some coffee? Water? Soda?" We both shook our heads and all three of us trooped down the hall to what I figured was an interrogation room. Sure enough, there was a table in the middle, with four chairs, and a big mirror on one of the algae-green walls. Brad closed the door behind us, and we all sat down. Both Mickey and I moved our chairs so that our backs were to the mirror. Brad smiled. "No worries. No one's behind there at the moment."

Mickey started. "Brad, we found out some information that we think is important."

"Good. Let's hear it."

Mickey looked at me and I shook my head to say that I would prefer not to do the talking. "Last night, before we all went out to dinner, Annabelle found a notepad in her bedroom. She rubbed her pencil over it and a name and phone number showed up. Georgia Browning. We found out…"

Brad held up his hand. "Stop." He paused and then leaned across the table toward me and frowned. "A notepad?" Where did you find it, exactly?"

"On the floor. Under the bed. Bonkers had been sitting on it."

Brad considered me briefly, then turned back to Mickey. "Go on."

Mickey hesitated. I think he was expecting Brad to ask why I hadn't said anything about this last night. At least, that's what I was expecting from Brad, but Brad just waited for Mickey to continue.

He did. "We located Georgia. She's a lawyer in San Francisco."

Brad closed his eyes and rubbed his forehead.

"Brad," I said, "I should have said something last night, but I was confused and upset and I didn't know who to trust, and, well…" My voice got quieter and quieter until I was practically rasping; I didn't finish the sentence. Brad frowned at both of us, back and forth.

"So, anyway," Mickey said, "we went to see Georgia Browning this afternoon. We knew that Cassie's lover was a lawyer, so we thought that might be the connection." Mickey's voice was a little muffled, too. He coughed.

Brad raised his eyebrows. "Her lover?"

"Yes," I said. "I didn't tell you that last night, that Cassie was gay." I sat on my hands.

Mickey continued. "But when Annabelle told Georgia what happened, she said she didn't know Cassie or anything about it, but she did seem upset and nervous." Brad's eyes widened and he nodded slightly.

"Yes. And we saw a picture in her office with her husband and kids. Well, we think that's who they were." I was whispering at this point.

Mickey jumped in. "But then we left, and on the way out I found a photograph on the front desk of residents of Tall Oaks, holding a banner thanking this woman Georgia, and Annabelle's grandmother and Mary Rosen were in the picture." Mickey pulled out his phone, found the picture he had taken, and held it up for Brad to see.

Brad stood up and walked over to the big two-way mirror. He placed his palms against it, stepped his feet back, and did a push-up or two against it. I could see his face reflected, and it was clear he was furious.

He came back and sat down. "So." His jaw was clenched. "Who do you think Georgia is?"

Mickey took a breath and exhaled through his mouth. It was my turn again. "We now know she's not Cassie's lover, because Mrs. Hobbs called me right after we left and I found out from her that Cassie's lover's name is Kirsten. No last name yet." I spit out that last sentence as fast as I could.

No one spoke for several moments. Then Brad leaned forward with his forearms on the table and studied Mickey, then me. "Do you understand what a murder investigation is?" I nodded. "Do you understand why it's not a good idea to withhold evidence?" I nodded again. He turned to Mickey. "Mickey, man, what were you thinking?" Mickey shook his head. "So, where is Ms. Browning? Did you leave her at her office?"

We told Brad that we did. Mickey gave him the address. Brad jotted it down on the back of one of his business cards, picked up the telephone, dialed an extension, and told it to whoever was on the other end of the line and asked them to locate a home address for Georgia Browning and to call him right back. He hung up the phone. "I'll send officers to both places."

"Brad." I had found my voice again. The worst of the confessional was over. "It may be that Cassie was going to contact Georgia about some legal issues, but I have to tell you, she was not a planner. She would not have been getting advice about wills or estates, which is what Georgia does. So the only thing I can think of is that Georgia called me for some reason, and Cassie answered the phone and wrote her name and number down, as a message."

Brad leaned back in his chair and pressed his fingertips together. "That sounds reasonable. Is it Cassie's handwriting?"

"I don't know. She's never written me a note or anything."

"Hmm. Well, maybe Georgia was scoping out your apartment, hoping to break in when no one would be there."

"But then why would she leave her name?" Mickey asked.

Brad shrugged. "People make mistakes like that all the time." He sneered. "People are stupid."

"Are you saying that you think Georgia murdered Cassie?"

Brad rose to his feet and hooked his thumbs in his belt. "I think Georgia's a suspect. That's all. Where's that notepad, by the way?"

I pulled it out of my pocket and handed it to Brad.

The phone rang, and Brad picked it up after he put the notepad in his inside jacket pocket. "Yeah. Got it. Good. Okay. Five minutes." He hung up. "We have a home address. I'm going there now and two uniforms will check out her office. You both can wait here, or I'll call you later." He walked over to the door and had his hand on the knob. "Annabelle, Beth Hobbs told me about Kirsten yesterday. I figured you knew she was gay when we had dinner last night. You're not helping by keeping information to yourself."

"Okay."

He opened the door. "We still only have a first name. If you think of any other information about how we might find Kirsten, you'll let me know, right?"

"Right," I said. *Maybe,* I thought.

Brad regarded me for a minute and then he left, closing the door behind him.

Mickey exhaled like he had been holding his breath for the last ten minutes. "I can't tell you how much better I feel now. We're on track. Brad will figure this out, even though he's a jerk. We can take a break."

"Mickey, he's more than a jerk. I heard him talking on the phone in his office. He beats up suspects. The chief of police is, in Brad's words, 'all over his ass.'"

Mickey frowned. "That's not good. Another loose cannon, like…"

"Jake? That's just what I was thinking."

Mickey rubbed his face. "Let's get a drink."

"Good idea. I think I'll have a kamikaze or a Long Island ice tea or a triple mindbender."

"What's a triple mindbender?"

"I have no idea. I don't drink any of those kinds of drinks. I made it up."

He smiled. "So, how about a glass of wine, or a glass of champagne, or…?"

"Nope. Single malt Scotch. Neat." I stood up. "I want to get to bed early, though. Tomorrow is going to be busy."

Mickey looked up at me. "It is? You're having breakfast with Mrs. Hobbs, right? What else?"

I rolled my eyes. "We're driving up to Tall Oaks tomorrow, remember?"

He stood up. "What?" He kind of yelled this.

"You heard me! We've talked about this! We're going to go up there and see what we can find out." I kind of yelled that.

"Annabelle! Goddammit, you just told Brad that you would let the police handle this. Don't you think he'll send someone up to Tall Oaks? You just basically promised him that you would stay out of this."

"I did no such thing! I told him that I'd let him know about any information I come up with! I didn't tell him I was going to crawl under a rock and not come out until he solves everything! We're talking about stuff that has to do with my *grandmother,* Mickey, my *grandmother.* My god, you're the one who suggested that she might have been murdered. I don't know, maybe that doesn't mean anything to you, maybe family is no big deal to you, but it is to me, and I'm not going to sit around and cry and not do anything."

Mickey had sat down again before I had reached the end of that speech. "Family is important, Annabelle. Surely you know that I know that."

I felt like a thoughtless dimwit. Mickey's parents were dead. He knew all about losing family. It was like I had just slapped him in the face. I sat down. "I'm sorry. I didn't mean that. God, I'm really sorry."

"It's okay."

"What about your grandparents? Did you know them? Are any of them still alive? Do you see them?"

"My grandfather, Poppy, lives in Scottsdale. He's an old right-wing Republican coot. Plays a lot of golf. Wears plaid pants. We send each other Christmas cards. He was my mother's father. She never liked him much either. My grandmother, my father's mom, is alive, too. She's in Maine, says the bitter winters keep her vigorous. I guess they do, too, because she's eighty-five and sturdy as a horse." Mickey stood up. "Annabelle, if we're going to Tall Oaks tomorrow, then I want to tell Brad, so it doesn't take him by surprise."

"Okay. I can live with that."

"Good. You know, you're a lot of wonderful things…"

"I hear a 'but' coming."

"But you're no private eye. You're too impulsive. You don't think things through. You don't hold back."

"Wait just a second, I'm the one who held back that note!" Mickey shook his head. "That was concealing evidence. I'm talking about strategizing, planning. You don't know how to do that very well, in my humble opinion."

"Your humble opinion as what? Are *you* a private eye?"

He looked shocked. "Of course not! But I'm a salesman. I know how to schmooze. I know how to draw people out. I know how to assess what someone wants or needs. I can sense when someone is hiding something."

"You didn't suss out that I was hiding that notepad."

"Oh, I knew something was up with you last night, I definitely did. But it's true that part of me figured you were just coping with the loss of your friend."

"So, are you saying that you want to do all the talking tomorrow when we go to Tall Oaks? That you'll do a better job?"

"That's right."

I don't like to be told I'm not good at something. At anything. Criticism isn't something that rolls off my shoulders. It sits there like a fifty-pound monkey. But I didn't feel like arguing. I just wanted to get out of there. So, I took a breath and said, "We'll see." Then I picked up my purse from the floor and marched to the door.

Mickey followed me. "Where do you want to get a drink?"

I stopped. "Palo Alto."

"Palo Alto? Isn't that far? Why Palo Alto?"

"There's a very comfy cozy living room there, well stocked with my favorite Scotch. It all belongs to Jeff and Sylvia Starkey, my parents."

Mickey shrugged. "Okay. Sure. Time to meet the parents. Will they be expecting us?"

"Let's surprise them."

On our way out I picked up Brad's business card and handed it to Mickey. "You should probably enter his number, too, on your cell phone."

"Already did. You keep it. You might need it."

I almost crumpled it up to toss it on the floor, thinking that I never wanted to need Brad Franklin for any reason ever again in my life. But instead I shoved it in my pants pocket, for Mickey's sake, and followed him out of the police station.

Chapter Fifteen

Mom and Dad live in a modest-size house by Palo Alto standards—the rich side of Palo Alto, that is—but it was always plenty big enough for the three of us. Twenty-five hundred square feet, with three bedrooms, and a lovely backyard that is meticulously groomed by my father on weekends. Shade trees surround it, and a low stone wall edges the back perimeter, draped with flowering vines. Dad plants bulbs every year. The blooms always seemed to be at their best in April and May, gigantic reds, whites, yellows, purples—you name it. And please do. I never inherited my father's knack for making things grow, and I never could keep the names of his flowers straight.

Mickey and I got to their house at about seven. I figured they'd be home, since generally Wednesday night is the one weeknight when one or the other isn't involved with some meeting for a volunteer community-minded organization, or a tennis game, or a hand of bridge, or a night shift. My father is a tenured professor at Stanford. Astrophysics. You'd never know it, just meeting him. You'd just as soon think he's a kindergarten teacher or a mailman. He's unassuming and gentle and generous. And Mom, well, she's a dynamo go-get-'em type, who has a hard time sitting still. She's an emergency-room doctor. She handles enormous stress on her job and puts up with a lot of wackos who come in off the street, drunk or angry or both. She's a tough cookie. I love and admire her, but when I'm in trouble, I usually end up confiding in Dad. He's more available.

My parents are good people. A little hard to live up to, though. They used to entertain visions of me finding the cure for cancer or proving the Big Bang Theory. Disappointed in me? They would never say so—I would. But I can rely on them, and they truly want me to be happy.

We rang the doorbell but before it opened I warned Mickey about my mother—"She swears like a sailor"—and then Mom answered with, "Honey! Holy crap! I didn't think you'd be back from Chicago yet!" Mickey let out a laugh.

Then Dad called from the den, "Muffinhead! Is that you?" Mickey looked at me and mouthed, "Muffinhead?" and I gave him my best go-ahead-make-my-day look.

Mom hugged me, after she took off my Giants baseball cap ("Bea, honey, I don't know why you hide under hats all the time"), then Dad hugged me, then I introduced Mickey to them both, and they all shook hands, and then Dusty, our old golden retriever ambled over and wiggled against everyone. Dad said, "Drink, anyone?" and Mickey said, "That's what we're here for," and everyone laughed.

We sat down in the den with our drinks. Mickey was drinking a gin and tonic, Mom and Dad had opened a bottle of Cabernet, and I was lingering over my Scotch. I began telling them about the last couple of days. Mom interrupted me a lot, with a lot of "why" questions and "holy shits," and Mickey would usually say, "We just don't know, Dr. Starkey." She finally said, "Oh for chrissakes, Mickey, call me Sylvia."

Dad was silent and listening intently. When I got to the part about Cassie being murdered, Mom yelled "Fuck!" and stood up abruptly, knocking her wine glass to the floor.

Mickey jumped up right away and touched her shoulder to calm her, while Dad went to the kitchen to get some baking soda and wet towels to mop up the spill.

I said, "Mom, I know, it's awful."

Mickey said, "Maybe you should sit back down, Sylvia." And she did.

Once we recovered from that, I got to the end of the story, right up to ringing their doorbell. I left out, by the way, any mention of romantic involvement with Mickey. I even lied about the suite in Las Vegas, mentioning that it had two bedrooms—it didn't—and said that we booked two rooms at the Sleep Tight Inn—we didn't—and that I had met Mickey previously at other book trade shows—I hadn't. I was trying to lie as charmingly and as successfully as Sandra Bullock in *While You Were Sleeping*—even though she was inventing a relationship whereas I was pretending not to have one. I didn't want them to have opinions about my flighty behavior, but I think Dad saw right through me. He gives me what I call his Gregory Peck look when he thinks I'm holding back—one eyebrow raised a bit, slight smile. He could have been rehearsing for *To Kill a Mockingbird*, with all of those Gregorys he was giving me.

When I finished, Mickey suggested that if we found a connection between Cassie, Georgia, and Nana, it could mean that Nana was murdered, too.

Mom paled. "Jeff, how can this be? We trusted Tall Oaks. Could she have been in such danger there?" My mother doesn't cry, but her eyes welled up.

Before Dad could answer, I emphasized that we didn't have any evidence of Nana being killed by anyone. I shot Mickey a warning glance to back off. It was the first time I had come to my mother's rescue. It was the first time she was the one who was crying.

Now it was after eight. Dad got up and went into the kitchen to order dinner, delivered from the local Italian restaurant. I was on my third Scotch, which is usually way too many for me, but it felt like I was just starting to relax.

"So, Mom, what about Nana at Tall Oaks? Can you remember anything weird going on there, or any people there who were creepy, like Mary Rosen?"

"I might recognize Mary, but I don't recall her now. No one struck me as creepy, though we did pack away Mother's good things a few months before she died, to make sure they were safe.

Should have done it sooner. We're lucky nothing was stolen."
She switched to Mickey. "Alzheimer's patients often don't know
what's theirs and what isn't." She smiled at Dad when he came
back to the den. "Remember, dear, we gave her a bunch of
plastic beads and costume jewelry, so that she could still dress
up and feel pretty? But her diamonds and good jewelry, no, we
have all of that here."

Mickey asked, "What about money? Or investments? Her
estate?"

Dad smiled. "Nothing there. Nana was a great old dame, and
part of her being a great old dame was that she never wanted
money, never cared about it, and managed to have what she
needed and basically nothing more. She gave a lot away. She
contributed to charities. We sold her house to move her into
Tall Oaks, and the sale took care of her expenses there. But she
really had nothing else."

A hush fell over us. It was like Nana was in the room, and
I found myself smiling at the thought. "One time, Mickey,
Nana found a twenty dollar bill on the street." Mom and Dad
shared a grin. "I was with her, about thirteen. She said, 'Oh my!
Some poor soul lost twenty dollars!' I said, 'Nana, it probably
wasn't some poor soul. It was probably someone who has lots of
money. People around here have lots of money.' She said, 'Well,
maybe so, but we can't know that, now, can we.' So we went to
the police station and she turned it over to the desk sergeant, in
case anyone came in looking for it. He thought she was crazy."

Mom said, "Yes, but it turned out she wasn't."

Mickey took the last swallow of his second gin and tonic.
"What happened?"

Mom sat up straight and crossed her legs. "The sergeant ended
up telling a reporter from the local newspaper about it, and the
reporter went to her house to interview her. The story was in
the paper that week, and by the end of the next week, Mother
had so many new students signing up for her ballroom dancing
classes that she had to add another class and hire a teacher to
help out. Her business took off."

"So, then she made some money?"

Dad leaned forward in his easy chair and put his forearms on his thighs. "Well, she could have, but it was the dancing and teaching that interested her, not the money. So if her students couldn't manage to pay, she wouldn't press them. And if her assistant teacher needed some help with a dentist bill or a babysitting bill, she'd pay."

"Lots of assholes took advantage of her," muttered Mom.

"She always gave a lot to the policeman's ball, too," I added.

"She had to!" Dad said. "She was usually a guest of honor and won I don't know how many citizen awards!" We all laughed at that.

Mickey reached his hand over to cover mine. "I wish I could have met her. What about Phyllis, her sister? Was she the same way?"

This took me by surprise. At first I thought, how does Mickey know about Phyllis? Then I remembered talking about Nana and Phyllis and Sara with Mary when we ate at The Full House in Las Vegas. Then I thought, damn, either he's got an awfully good memory or he's been keeping notes.

"Phyllis," my mother answered, "was a sweet woman with not a lot of brain power. She was younger than my mother, and my mother looked after her a lot when they were growing up. She died young, around fifty-five, I think."

"She had money." Dad was pouring himself another glass of wine. "She married well, an entrepreneur who built up a nice small chain of restaurants in the Midwest and then sold them for a pretty penny."

"Uncle Doug. He died, when, Dad, last year?"

"Two years now, I think. Is that right, Sylvia?"

"Mmm. I think so. Sara had a nice inheritance, which will keep her well for the rest of her life, especially in Omaha."

Mickey said, "Sara is your cousin, then, is that right?"

"That's right."

"Well, I don't think Phyllis and Doug and Sara have anything to do with this mess with Nana," I said. "The last thing we need is to pull another city and state into the mix. Who knows anything about Omaha anyway? Lots of steaks. Wheat. Cows. Before they're steaks, that is."

Dad smiled. "You seemed to think Iowa was all right for a time."

"Yup, I did." I looked at Mickey and said, "I went to Coe College in Cedar Rapids," then turned back to Dad. "I think Nebraska is all right, too. I'm just not sure a bad cop in Las Vegas has any interest in anything going on in Omaha."

The doorbell rang—dinner had arrived—and Mom jumped up to get it, almost toppling her wine glass again, but Mickey's quick reflexes caught the glass before it tipped too far. Quick reflexes, sharp memory, good hair, and easy around parents. I don't know why I was feeling funny about him then. Maybe he was just too perfect.

◇◇◇

We continued talking about Nana and Tall Oaks and Cassie's murder through dinner, but Mom and Dad couldn't come up with anything that might connect Nana to everything else that had happened. In fact, they seemed sure that there couldn't be a connection between Cassie's murder and Nana. I couldn't blame them. It was all too wacky. They had never heard of Georgia Browning, either.

We finished dinner around ten, and that's when Mickey's cell phone rang. He excused himself and went out on the back deck. Mom pinched me after he had closed the sliding glass door behind him.

"Ouch!"

"So what about him! Hubba hubba!"

I rolled my eyes. "Hubba HUBba?? *Huh?* Well, what *about* him?" I did my best to sound indignant.

"Come on, Bea, is he a boyfriend? Are you sleeping together?" I looked at Dad imploringly, but he just raised his eyebrows at me, all Gregory Pecky again.

"Mom, jeez, we seem to like each other, and he has been very good to me through all of this. He's good at taking care of people, I think, and…"

"...and he's in love with you." This came from Dad, and it took me off guard. "It's clear, muffinhead, I knew it as soon as you both walked in the door."

My mother clapped her hands together and said, "No shit!"

I rolled my eyes again, but I felt my ears get hot, which meant they were glowing like halogen lightbulbs. I tried to act annoyed, but I found myself grinning. "You guys, really, stop, I mean it."

Mickey came back in, and we all picked up our forks like we had been eating non-stop since he left, even though there was no more food left on anyone's plate. "That was Brad." We all put our forks down and looked at him. "They checked out Georgia Browning's office. She wasn't there. They went to her home, and she wasn't there, either. In fact, no one was there. So they talked to neighbors next door. Georgia and her husband were separated last year, and she moved into her flat when they split up."

"And he kept the kids?"

"The neighbors said she didn't have any kids."

"So who were those kids in the picture?"

"The receptionist said they were Georgia's husband's nephews. Anyway, they found out the make of her car and they'll keep looking for her. They've also cracked Cassie's password protection on her laptop and found some emails from a Kirsten Day. They've located her and are questioning her." He paused. "There's something else, Annabelle. Georgia used to be the legal consultant at a Las Vegas casino. She moved to San Francisco only about a year ago and hung a shingle as an estate lawyer."

I took a deep inhale. "So she could easily know Jake."

Mickey nodded.

"Did you tell Brad about our planned trip tomorrow?"

"Yes. Surprisingly, he didn't seem too concerned about it. I think he believes that Tall Oaks has little to do with anything, or, at least, it's not a priority in this investigation. I did promise him we would tell him about anything we find out."

"It's not a good idea, Mick." Dad stood up and looked from one of us to the other. "Bea, I don't want you to have anything more to do with any of this. You've been kidnapped, your friend has been killed, your hotel rooms and your apartment ransacked. This isn't some great adventure. It's dangerous, and it's time you left it all to the police."

"A-fucking-men, darling," said Mom.

"I understand, Jeff," said Mickey, "and the only reason I'm going along is to do my best to look after Annabelle." All three of them looked at me.

"Look. We're just going up to Tall Oaks. In broad daylight. The police already know what's going on, both in Las Vegas and San Francisco. I don't have to be back at work until Monday. I don't see how I can do anything else except try to figure this out. I'll go crazy if I don't."

"Sweetie," Mom said, "aren't you scared? Because I am. We are. And let's face it, you're not equipped to take this on."

I stiffened. "If I'm doing something, then I'm not sitting around and being scared, and that means I'm less scared. I like to be in control, you know that." I appealed to my father. "Dad, I don't want you to worry, even though I know you will. Mickey and I will be careful. I promise. Really, I have to do this."

Dad took my hand. "Muffin, it's not up to you to fix this. It wasn't up to you last year, and it's not up to you now. Give yourself a break."

I shook my head. "I have to do this."

"What happened last year?" Mickey asked.

The three of them were staring at me, waiting. I sighed. "It was at the company's holiday dinner. The computer tech guy got really drunk. I went to the ladies' room and found him there, trying to rape Carol, our customer service manager."

"Jesus. What did you do?"

"She grabbed the fucking asshole and pulled him off and called security!" Mom put her hand on my shoulder. "You did everything you could, honey."

"No, I didn't. Carol decided not to press charges, and I conveniently let the whole thing go."

"Because she *asked* you to let the whole thing go." Dad sat back down.

"I could have tried to get counseling for her, I could have even pressed assault charges myself on him since he pushed me away after I got him off of her."

Mickey looked confused. "I don't get it. The woman didn't want your help. So why are you beating yourself up about this?"

I took a breath. "Nice choice of words. The guy beat *her* up a week later. She was in the hospital for four days."

"She's okay? And the asshole is in jail now?"

I took a deeper breath. "She's okay. The asshole as far as I know, however, is still working freelance, servicing computer systems, and making a good living."

"As far as you know." Mickey paused. "This asshole, what's his name?"

"Jerry Walbon." As soon as I said it, a little shiver ran down my spine. "You don't think…"

"He might be carrying a grudge. Might have been looking for you and killed Cassie instead."

Mom said, "Oh, fuck," and brought her hand up to her mouth, like she was going to start crying again.

I put my hand on her shoulder. I was starting to warm to our role reversals. "I don't know. I think he left town. He got away with it, so why would he come back after me?"

Mickey frowned. "Carol never pressed charges?"

"Well, she did, but then changed her mind. Quit her job. Moved away."

"So, Walbon got away with assault, and that's why now you want to nail a bad guy."

"Mickey, I want someone, the right someone, to pay for Cassie's murder. I'm involved, like I was before, but I can't sit by this time and just hope for justice for my friend."

"It's not very smart, but I get it. We should tell Brad about Walbon in any case."

Dad sighed. "You call us every day. If we don't hear from you by seven every night, I call the police. Understood?"

"Absolutely. Yes." I took Brad's business card out of my pocket and gave it to him.

"Shit. I don't like this at all." Mom stood up. "Maybe we should go with you?"

"You have work tomorrow." I got up and hugged her. "It'll be okay, Mom. Really. Go to bed now."

She squeezed me and then let me go. "Well, all right, after I put these dishes in the dishwasher. Why don't you both stay here tonight."

Dad walked around the table and put his arm around me. "Yes, in fact, I insist that you stay here. You've had too much to drink to drive, and you both look spent."

I raised my eyebrows at Mickey and he gave an it's-all-right-with-me shrug. "Okay, thanks, we will. I'll stay in my old room on the futon, and Mickey can sleep on the foldout in the den."

Mom smiled. "Whatever, honey." My ears lit up again.

"But we'll do the dishes," said Mickey. "Really, you've been so hospitable, let us clean up, and the two of you can go to bed."

"Thanks, good idea." Dad gave Mickey a man-slap on his back and motioned toward Mom with his head toward the stairs.

"Good night!" Mom whispered, with a wink, and they left us.

We picked up the plates, bowls, and silverware, and took them into the kitchen. I started rinsing them in the sink, but Mickey just started putting everything right into the dishwasher. "Mickey! You have to rinse them first!"

"No you don't." He took everything then, at warp speed, and piled it into the dishwasher, opened the cupboard beneath the sink, while scooting me to the side with his hip, found the dishwasher soap, poured it in the right place, closed the door, latched it, and turned the machine on. Then he grabbed a sponge and wiped down the counters, rinsed the sponge, wiped off the dining room table, and tossed the sponge into the sink. Then he grabbed me around my waist, pulled me to him, and kissed me hard. Any funny feelings I had about him earlier vanished. I threw my arms around his neck and my legs around his waist; he held me tightly, still kissing me, and walked into the den. I let go with my legs and Mickey gently pushed me onto the couch on my back, lay on top of me, and kept kissing me. He was grinding his pelvis into me, and I was giving it back. I flashed on Keira Knightly again, this time in *Atonement* when James McAvoy has sex with her against the wall in her family's mansion. I don't think I had ever wanted a man so much in my life. I mean Mickey, of course, not James McAvoy, though I think he's way hot.

We broke apart to start taking our clothes off.

"This is nuts!" I whispered.

"Why?" He was practically ripping his pants off, trying to undo the top button.

"We're in my parents' house! They'll hear us! They'll come down for a drink of water, or something, and see us! And Dusty is asleep right over there!" I was struggling to undo my bra.

"We'll be very very quiet. We already know how to do that! And Dusty won't mind."

I started giggling. We were both standing up now, hopping around on one foot and then the other, pulling our pants off, our underwear. "Should I pull out the couch, turn it into a bed?"

"No time!" And Mickey had me down again, and you would have thought we hadn't seen each other for about a hundred years, the way we held on tight, every place we could hold on to each other. But we weren't so successful being quiet this time, and when I didn't know anything anymore except the waves of bliss pulsing through my body, I let out a moan loud enough to wake up old Dusty, who answered me with a bark, and then Mickey emitted some sort of ecstatic yell. As we were falling asleep wrapped up in each other on that couch, I could have sworn I heard my parents laughing upstairs.

Chapter Sixteen

I woke up early, around six, extricated myself from Mickey, and stood there surveying the wreckage. I picked up clothing, piece by piece. Dusty had shifted position during the night and was curled up with my black jeans, which didn't look very black anymore, as they were sporting a goodly amount of dog hair and a few traces of dog spittle. She stood up and wagged her tail, looking at me. I scratched her head. "Good morning, girl. Good girl."

I walked back over to the couch. "Psst!" Mickey didn't move. "Mickey, hey!" I was speaking softly. He still didn't move. I dropped the pile of clothes on his head. Still nothing. Then Dusty started licking the bottom of his right foot. That did it.

Mickey sat up in a hurry. The clothes spilled over him, onto the floor. "What the...?" He looked up at me. "Were you licking my feet?"

"You wish. Get up. I don't want my parents to find us naked on this couch." I reached out my arm to him.

He swung his legs over the side of the couch, took my hand, and hauled himself up. "Good morning, beautiful." He smiled. I smiled. We kissed.

"There's a shower in the downstairs bathroom, down the hall toward the back of the house. Dad uses it to clean up after gardening. There should be some clean towels in there." I kissed him again, and he headed down the hallway. I picked up the clothes again and sorted them into his and mine on the couch. Then I grabbed my bundle and tiptoed upstairs to my old bedroom, went inside, and shut the door.

Mom had turned this into her office once I had left home for good. It was cozy and neat. The walls were covered with family pictures, going back to her great grandparents. I walked over to a group of photographs of Nana that documented her life: a baby picture; one with her sister, their arms about each other's shoulders; her wedding portrait; another when she must have been about sixty. My eyes lingered on this one, taking in her vigor and bright eyes. The last picture was one of Nana at Tall Oaks, sitting in the common area where the residents sing songs, make crafts, watch movies. She was in a wheelchair, but she was smiling and the flat palms of her hands were pressed together. She had been clapping to some music, I knew.

I looked around at the other stuff in Mom's office and smiled when I saw Nana's old clock, sitting on top of some bookshelves. It was the one I retrieved from Tall Oaks after Nana died. Mom wanted to figure out how to get it going again. Dad told her to take it somewhere to have it fixed, or to have the moving parts replaced. But she was adamant about learning how to do it herself. It was a pretty cathedral clock, about eighteen inches high, with an elegantly painted face. Its "door" closed with a small brass latch and had clear glass in front of the face, with decorative, opaque glass beneath that, so that you couldn't really see the pendulum.

"Maybe if you stare at it long enough, then it will start." I turned to see Mom standing in the doorway. "It's worth a try, anyway." She smiled.

"Hi, Mom. I was just about to take a shower."

"Go ahead, honey. I'll get coffee started. I don't have to be at the hospital until eleven, so take your time." She paused. "Annabelle, Nana could have been smothered. There was no autopsy. We didn't ask for one. Her body had been slowly shutting down, and the doctor saw no reason to alert the coroner."

"Mom…"

"Don't put yourself in harm's way. I don't want to bury you, too." She turned and headed downstairs. I hoped she didn't find Mickey as naked as she had found me.

About an hour later, all four of us were gathered around the dining room table again, cradling mugs of coffee and reading various sections of the paper. Dad had taken Dusty for a walk around the neighborhood, and Mom had an Entenmann's coffee cake in the oven. I peeked up at all of them, so at ease with each other and with me, and in that moment, everything felt so good. Dad looked up at me and grinned. Then we both went back to the paper.

While we were eating coffee cake and still reading, Mom disappeared for a bit, then showed up with a shoebox in hand. She put it on the table in front of me. I knew right away what was in it: Nana's jewelry. I looked up at her. Dad and Mickey put the paper down.

"I've been thinking about this box ever since last night," she said. "You know Mother didn't have much, but it just doesn't make sense to keep these things hidden away. I guess I didn't think I was ready to look at them, that they would make me too fucking sad." She looked at Mickey. "Sorry, I swear like Chris Rock." Mickey put his hand up in a little wave to signal it was okay with him. Mom sat down next to me and opened the box. "But now I want to look at them, and I want you to have something."

"Wow." I pulled out a string of pearls, almost pink in color. "Turn around, Mom." She shifted in her chair, and I brought the pearls around her neck and fastened them. She turned back, fingering the shiny beads.

"I'm not sure they are the perfect accessory for your bathrobe, but they're stunning on you."

Mom turned slightly to face Dad, and he smiled at her. "Lovely."

There were a couple of bracelets, an amethyst pendant, a silver brooch, and about a half dozen pairs of earrings. Nana wasn't flashy, and mostly she wore inexpensive jewelry. These were her "good" pieces. We delighted in each of them as we laid them out on the table. Then Mom pulled out a small box, and opened it. She took out a ring, and held it out to me. "I want you to have this, Bea."

My eyes immediately filled up, remembering that ring on Nana's finger, and before I took it I threw my arms around Mom and hugged her close. Then I put the ring on the little finger of my right hand, which happened to be one of only a few of my fingers that didn't already sport a ring. It fit perfectly. I knew it would. I used to try this ring on when I would visit Nana, before she moved to Tall Oaks. It was a gold initial ring, with two very tiny diamonds on either side of the oval where Nana's initials were engraved. Her husband had given it to her for her thirtieth birthday; it had "ILYT" inside, for "I Love You Truly." It had been one of Nana's favorite possessions.

I held up my hand to my father, and, softie that he is, his eyes had teared up, too, watching me. He just nodded. Then I held out my hand to Mickey, and he took it in both of his and examined the ring. "Nice. Very nice."

Mom was pulling the last few things out of the shoebox: a couple of watches, a ruby pin, and a gaudy beaded glasses case. She held this up and said, "Remember this?"

I took it from her. "Yes. She used it all the time. It's pretty raggedy now. I fingered the velvet case in my hands. "See how some of these things are coming through the other side? The material is really worn." I fiddled with the baubles some more. "This piece is really loose." I pulled it out and held it up.

"Looks like a hatpin to me," Mom said.

The pin sported a two-inch pretty enamel oval, designed with rich blue and purple swirls surrounding a gold bird, which had a glittery diamond for an eye. It seemed to be pure gold. I turned it over and confirmed out loud, "Fourteen carats." Then I looked closer at the back, and sat up straight. "Tarcelloni!" It was engraved with the brand name, as well as another scripty scribble I couldn't make out.

The three of them looked at me. "What?" asked Mickey.

"Tarcelloni! Hat designer! Mary Rosen! She was wearing a Tarcelloni hat!"

"Do you think this is her hatpin?"

I jumped up. "Holy bejesus, yes, she even said something in the elevator about keeping her hat on without it. Maybe this is worth some incredible amount of money, and that's what all of this fuss is about!" I was getting riled up. "This is it. This is what everyone's looking for—it has to be! Remember, Mickey, my stick pin was missing from my jewelry case? Maybe there has been some sort of mix-up with pins!"

"I don't know, Annabelle." Mickey took the hatpin and turned it over in his hand. "It doesn't seem very valuable."

"Wait!" Mom stood up. "I remember Mary Rosen! Hats. She was the woman who wore the fancy hats. I used to see her, pass her on the porch or the stairs, when I would visit Mother."

I grabbed Mom's arm. "What did she say? What do you remember?" Mickey stood up, too. Dad, the sanest one of us, stayed seated.

"We never talked, really. We would say hello, and comment on the weather. I wasn't used to having any sort of real conversations with residents there, so it's not like I was seeking her, or anyone else, out. But let me think." Mom sat back down. So did I. So did Mickey. Dusty came over to Dad and put her head in his lap, and he scratched her behind her ears.

"Okay. There was one conversation. I said something about it being a nice day, and she said, yes it was, and I asked her if she was expecting any visitors, because she had such a lovely hat and outfit on, and she said yes, she was hoping to meet with her lawyer that day."

I rubbed my hands together. "Her lawyer! This is great. It had to be Georgia Browning. They know each other."

Dusty let out a little bark and trotted over and sat down next to me, looking up. Excitement in the house. Another walk coming up, maybe.

Dad was not a man who warmed to outbursts. "Bea, there are lots of lawyers in the world, and probably several others beside

Georgia Browning visited Tall Oaks. In any case, you've already told us about the connection between Tall Oaks and Georgia, and both Mary and Georgia were in that photograph in Georgia's office, so I'm not sure this is a big deal."

I looked at Mickey. "Maybe not," he said, and then turned to Dad. "But if it *was* Georgia, then we know that Georgia and Mary had conversations with each other, and that means we've connected a few more dots. Georgia is connected somehow to Annabelle's apartment. Mary, maybe, is connected to Georgia. Georgia, maybe, is connected to Jake. Mary somehow ended up with us in Las Vegas." He stopped, looking momentarily unsure of himself.

"Yes!" I shouted. Dusty barked. "It has to be the hatpin. I don't know how it ended up on Nana's glasses case, but maybe Mary thought I had it." I paused and then snapped my fingers. "She looked through my purse, when we got out of the taxi, remember, Mickey? I thought she was going for my wallet, but maybe she was looking for the glasses case."

"Maybe. But…"

"No buts! I feel sure about this!"

"BUT, Annabelle, how did the glasses case end up in the shoebox with Nana's good jewelry? I thought she only had fake stuff at Tall Oaks."

"I can answer that," Mom said. "When Bea gave me everything she packed up from Mother's room, I went through the plastic beads and other trinkets and got rid of most of it, but I saved a couple of things—this watch," she picked it up, "which is a cheapo, but it's cute, and the glasses case. I tossed them both in this box."

I was so glad to have this lead. It made me feel grounded, like we were on the right track, or at least any track at all. "Mickey, let's go. Bring the hatpin with you. I want to get up to Tall Oaks. And we have to stop and feed Bonkers. And I need to change my clothes. And, oh crap! What time is it? I'm supposed to meet Mrs. Hobbs at ten. Mom, Dad, thanks for a great visit. Dusty!" She stood up and was wiggling all over now. "You're a good good girl!" I squatted and hugged her. "Dad, she needs another walk I think."

"Gee, muffinhead, thanks for cluing me in." Dad stood up and went to get Dusty's leash, gave me a kiss on the cheek—"Be careful"—and called Dusty to the back door.

"Thanks, Mom." I hugged her and grabbed my purse from the kitchen counter.

"You call, honey, you keep us informed. Don't do anything rash. Don't take chances. Mickey, you take care of her."

"Will do, Sylvia. Thanks for everything. Great to meet you." Mickey held out his hand, but Mom gave him a hug instead.

"Oh for fuck's sake, Mickey, you're practically family now." She let him go and gave him a wink, and Mickey and I headed out the door.

Chapter Seventeen

Bonkers was right by the front door to my apartment when Mickey and I got there. He was rubbing against my legs as soon as I stepped in, and I swooped him up in my arms. "Bonkers boo, I love you. How are you, my excellent kitty?" I gave him a few kisses and put him down. Then I went into the kitchen to feed him. I heard Mickey say, "Hey there, cat. Yeah, good cat. Yeah...Yow! Stop it!" He walked in, sucking on his hand.

"Jesus, Annabelle, Bonkers just bit me!"

"He thinks men like that kind of thing. He's just playing. Get a Band Aid, that cupboard right there." I pointed, and Bonkers started rubbing against Mickey's legs. Mickey looked down at him and growled. Bonkers split.

After I fed Bonks, I cleaned out his litter box and changed my clothes, opting for a black cotton beret this time—it doesn't cover up my ears, but I think it makes them look smaller—to go with my black cotton capri pants and black t-shirt, while Mickey sat in the living room and turned on CNN. The place was still a disaster. It reminded me of the final scene of *The Conversation,* except that Gene Hackman had torn apart his own place, looking for a bug, the listening-device, I mean, and at least my floorboards were still intact. Anyway, I wanted to get out of there as soon as we could. It cranked up my anxiety to an all-time high. I was certain we were on the verge of finding the explanation for this insanely terrifying situation. I couldn't stand any more murderers, kidnappers, thieves, or liars. I even yearned for my boring life back.

I checked my messages, but there weren't any. This made me remember my new cell phone, so I pulled it out of my purse and checked that voice mail. "No new messages," said the automaton-like voice.

"Mickey!" I called from the bedroom.

"Yeah."

"Luis, have you heard from Luis?"

"No."

"Don't you think we should have heard from him by now?"

"Well, he probably has a lot going on with his captain, and I bet if he had found out anything more to tell us, he would have called."

I walked into the living room. "I think we should check in with him. I'm going to call him."

Mickey was standing at my desk, sifting through a pile of papers. He looked up and blurted out, "No!" We froze for a few seconds eyeing each other.

"What are you doing?"

"Just straightening out some stuff." He patted the desk. "But don't call Luis. We shouldn't bother him. He'll call us."

Nothing about Mickey seemed perfect in that moment. I didn't like him snooping around my stuff. I didn't like it that he didn't want me to call Luis—not now, and not when we were in the car. Marilyn Monroe once said, "A wise girl kisses but doesn't love, listens but doesn't believe, and leaves before she is left." I wanted to run. Maybe Mickey was using me for some reason, and had been ever since Chicago. Maybe our chance encounter wasn't by chance at all. I could be dead wrong about him.

"What's the big deal? If I want to call Luis, I'll call Luis. I want to know how he's doing, anyway. I mean, maybe he's in trouble now, too. Why shouldn't we call him?"

Mickey was jittery, kind of rocking back and forth, left to right. He ran his hand through his hair. Then he looked at his watch. "It's 9:45. You're going to be late to see Mrs. Hobbs."

I stared at him. My stomach churned and I figured the buffaloes would be showing up any minute. I didn't know what was
up with Mickey, but I didn't want to be talking to Luis now with
Mickey acting all secret-agent-man. I'd call him later. I put my
phone in my pocket and grabbed my purse. "Are you coming
with me? Or do you want to meet later to go up to Tall Oaks?"

"I'll drive you to the café where you're meeting her and drop
you off. I'll pick you up at eleven. I have to go back to the hotel
and change and check my emails."

"Fine."

I gave Bonkers a last hug, and Mickey and I left the apartment. San Francisco is usually cool in June, but right then, it
felt like a flash blizzard had just hit my city. I was cold all over.

Chapter Eighteen

We didn't speak on the way to the café. When Mickey pulled up to the curb to let me off, I got out without a word. I walked toward the door, but I stopped and turned around after he had taken off. I watched the Mustang head down Bush Street, then it pulled over again, then it stopped. Mickey didn't get out.

I pulled out my phone and called Luis. It rang once and switched over to voicemail. Either he was busy with another call and not answering mine, or his phone was turned off. Could Mickey have Luis on the phone right now? I dropped my phone in my jacket pocket, and headed in to meet Beth Hobbs.

I knew it was her the minute I saw her—she was the only middle-aged woman in the place, already seated at a table, nursing a cup of coffee. As I walked over, she noticed me and stood up. "Annabelle?" I greeted her with a hug.

I think of myself as a pretty nice person, basically compassionate, and while not generous to a fault, at least open-minded and essentially nonviolent. But two things were going on during that coffee klatch. One, I was preoccupied with Mickey's odd behavior, and two, I took an immediate dislike to Mrs. Hobbs. First off, her hug was limp. Then, as soon as we ordered coffee from the hovering waiter, her phone rang and she pulled it right out with no apology, and spoke into it, "Yes." Pause. "Right." She disconnected, put the phone down on the table, and looked at me. "I don't have a lot of time, Annabelle. It has been a very hard couple of days, as I'm sure you understand. So why don't you tell me everything you know? You're not involved in my daughter's murder, are you?"

Okay. Deep breath. I understood that she was in shock, and sad beyond description, and angry, and all of that, and really, I could have let that comment go. My problem was that she was too cool and too calm. And then there was her lipstick. It was a god-awful orange, and I won't lie, that color alone would have warned me off anyone sitting across a table from me. I don't trust orange lipstick. Except maybe on Anne Hathaway, who could wear any color on her face and still have the screen presence of Elizabeth Taylor. But all that aside, I remembered a story, looking at those lips, that Cassie had told me about her mother on one of our walks. We were chatting about dieting and exercise and fashion and make-up and how our women-must-look-a-certain-way society was insulting and depressing and just plain wrong. Then Cassie laughed and said that one of the things she loved about her mother was that she never wore make-up, except for Cherries in the Snow red lipstick. She never left the house without it.

So there I sat, freaking out inside, wondering, again, what the hell was going on. My heart started racing, the buffaloes were stampeding in my innards. I couldn't speak until she prodded me. "Well, don't you have anything to say?" She pressed her lips together.

That raised my hackles—although I have no idea what hackles are—even further, and my bravado prevailed. "Show me your identification, lady, and do it quick before I shove your iPhone down your throat."

She acted shocked but not really, if you know what I mean— she never would have made it as an actor. Really, worse than Andie McDowell, who, if you ask me, couldn't act her way out of a Cialis commercial. "How dare you," she simmered, or tried to simmer, while she snatched her iPhone.

I grabbed her wrist before it left the table. "Where's Beth Hobbs?"

"Let go of me. Now."

I didn't let go. Instead, I took her purse with my other hand and shook it upside down on the table. Her wallet fell out and I picked it up. It wasn't a wallet at all. It was a badge holder. This lady was a cop. I let go.

"Jeez. This is the best the SFPD can do? Detective Nancy Mellon? You thought I would reveal some deep, dark secret, thinking that you were Beth Hobbs? Do you know who Andie McDowell is? Because even SHE would have done a better job!" I stood up.

Officer Mellon stood up, too. "Surprise. I'm no Andie McDowell. Sit down, Annabelle."

I rolled my eyes and stalked out. Mickey wasn't due to pick me up for another forty-five minutes, but there was the Mustang, still parked down the street.

Mellon came out of the café. "Look, Annabelle, Brad and Mick figured you might want to reveal something to Beth Hobbs that you wouldn't feel comfortable telling the police. You're right, I blew it. But if you're holding anything back, now might be the time to tell me."

I stared at her. "Brad and Mick? Brad and MICK? Do you mean Brad and MICKEY PAXTON?"

She nodded. "Yes. Detective Mick Paxton."

"He's a DETECTIVE??" I was backing away from her then, away from the café, and away from the Mustang.

"Annabelle, come on, let's go back in and talk."

I was already turning to run, one block over to Sutter Street, and then down the hill, finding it hard to breathe, and wishing I could fly.

After a couple of blocks I turned right on Grant and then a left on Post and ducked into Gumps. If you don't know Gumps, make sure you go there on your next trip to San Francisco. It's full of exquisite, expensive objects, from Japanese painted scrolls to framed exotic bugs to hand-engraved fine crystal cake platters that would be perfect for a cozy dinner for eighteen, served by a maid showing off Schwarzenegger biceps in order to lift them.

Upstairs features custom Asian-style furniture—red-lacquer chests, bamboo chairs, ceramic garden stools—among some odd designer pieces. That's where I darted and plopped down on an overstuffed zebra-printed ottoman, hoping, even at that anxiety-filled moment, that it was faux zebra. I consider animals God's creatures; we humans are supposed to be learning things from them, not turning them into comfy footrests.

I dropped my head between my knees and tried to slow my breathing. *Sea of Love* came rushing back to me, and I sure didn't want to be in that movie anymore. Ellen Barkin didn't know that Al Pacino was a cop, either, let alone that he thought she was a murderer. Maybe it wasn't such a great film after all.

Then Kevin came up and softly laid his hand on my shoulder. I knew he was Kevin because he said, "Miss, I'm Kevin Morgan, furniture sales associate. May I help you with something?"

I didn't sit up. I shook my head and mumbled, "No, thanks." Then I heard Mickey.

"Thanks, Kevin. My wife and I are simply having a little disagreement on the price of a new chair. If you can give us a few minutes, I'm sure we'll work this out quietly."

"Certainly, sir, take your time, and let me know if I can be of any assistance." Kevin walked away. Mickey's nice Cole Hahns stood on the floor in front of my feet. He squatted down. I still didn't sit up.

"Annabelle, let's get out of here."

I shook my head.

"I saw you run. I was looking in the rear-view mirror."

I didn't move.

"I saw you talking to Officer Mellon. I guess she told you…"

I still didn't twitch one muscle.

Mick reached out to brush my hair back from my face. I swatted his hand. "Don't touch me."

"I had to lie to you."

I snorted. "Really. All day long, every day since we met, or what?" That's when I straightened up and faced him. "You bastard."

Mickey rose. "Everything was the truth, except the part about my being a sales rep. Everything else was true. Everything, Annabelle." He sat down on a leopard-print stool next to me, or maybe it was cheetah. Who would buy such a thing?

My eyes drilled into his. "And you didn't tell me because…?"

He sighed. "I was undercover in Chicago. On a completely unrelated case. I didn't want to bring you into that, or to have this whole catastrophe mixed up with that."

I kept aim on his eyes. "I'm listening." See? Remember what I said about being open-minded and compassionate? That was me at this moment, even though I was preparing myself to jump up, punch him in the nose, and throw the zebra chair over the railing onto the fancy crystal platters below.

"I was at the book convention to investigate a matter that has nothing to do with books but everything to do with the convention center and the union. An extortion case. Then I met you, and the convention was over, and I had gotten the information I needed, and like I said"—he gave me a tentative smile—"I met you."

"Hmm. And when we were being chased all over hell and my roommate is murdered and you meet my parents, for god's sake, it didn't occur to you that you should tell me the truth? And then you set me up, Mickey, you SET ME UP, to meet a cop with orange smackers who couldn't act her way out of a Cialis commercial?"

"What?"

"How could you send me off to that meeting this morning, knowing what was going on?"

Mickey reached for my hand, but I pulled it away from him. "How?"

"I didn't like it."

I turned my head away from him.

"I didn't like it, Annabelle, but Brad told me that they had to confirm if you are involved in all of this, and you can see his point, really, that they had to make sure you weren't hiding anything, even though I told him I was sure you weren't. So he came up with this plan and I went along with it, because if I didn't, he wasn't going to trust me, either."

I let my mouth fall open. "You're kidding me, Mickey. How can cops be this stupid, to try a harebrained plan like this?"

He tried his little smile again. "Brad was never the brightest guy at the academy, and Detective Mellon, well, who knew she was a worse actress than Andie McDowell?"

"You heard me tell her that?"

"Tell her what?"

"The Andie McDowell thing? You said that on your own?"

He wrinkled his forehead. "I wasn't hooked up to any listening device."

"Oh jeez. How can it be that I have found this man who likes *Silverado* and doesn't like Andie McDowell, and whose pants are basically a great fit, only to find out that he's a big fat liar?" I sprang off the ottoman.

"I'm with you in this thing. Really, I am."

"I don't want you in this thing anymore."

"That doesn't matter too much at this point."

"ExCUSE me?" I was ready to punch him now.

"I'm basically assigned to you. I promised Brad I'd stick with you. Otherwise, he'll bring you into the station for a long spell of questioning, and you won't make it up to Tall Oaks."

It was a face off. Sergio Leone's theme music from *The Good, The Bad, and The Ugly* would have provided the perfect backdrop.

"Mickey, where do you live?"

"New York. I told you, I didn't lie about anything else."

"How come you have so much money?"

"Parents. Had a lot. Died young, left me with, well, a small fortune." He rubbed the back of his neck nervously.

"You told me that your dad was a plumber and your mom a hair stylist."

"That wasn't a lie. Just not the whole truth. Dad was an inventor of sorts, too. Came up with a new pipe sealant, sold the patent to WaterWorks Tools for a pile of dough."

"Fuck you, Mickey. How much else have you told me that's 'just not the whole truth'?" My voice had risen, and Kevin started walking toward us again, but I half waved at him and mouthed that I was sorry, making the motion of zipping my lips. He leaned against a bamboo secretary—a desk, not a person—and stayed there, keeping an eye on us.

"I know. Fuck me. I know. I handled this badly. I was trying to keep my cover, I had to try to figure out what was happening in Las Vegas, I had to figure you out, I..."

"Why were you looking through papers on my desk this morning?"

He paused. "Bad habit. Murder scene. Papers all over your desk. I'm a detective. I shouldn't have done that. I wasn't thinking."

"Do you think I'm involved in this? Do you think I'm one of the bad guys?"

He didn't smile. "I know you're not."

"How do you know?"

"I saw you tie up a guy with dental floss. I caught you when you collapsed when you heard about Cassie. I met your parents. I met your cat." He paused. "I made love with you." He paused again. "I'm *in* love with you."

"Really." Then I punched in him in the face. My fist didn't land squarely—I haven't practiced punching in a long time, basically since my eleven-year-old attack on the kid next door—and he dodged it, but I got the side of his nose well enough that he yelled "Ow!"

I turned on my heel and marched toward the stairs. "Kevin, we're leaving. My husband would like to purchase that cheetah bench there. Cost is no issue. In fact, he wants ten of them. Charge his VISA. I mean his American Express."

"Have a wonderful day," replied Kevin, while Mickey followed me out, holding his nose with one hand and apologetically waving at Kevin with his other, his credit cards safe in his wallet.

Chapter Nineteen

On the drive up to Santa Rosa, Mickey couldn't seem to shut up. Not that I wanted him to, particularly. I was driving, even though he told me at least four times that I wasn't on the rental car agreement and this meant we would be in big trouble if I got into an accident. I reminded him of the mountain lion fetish I had in my pocket, and how it had protected me so well up until now, and surely it would take care of me on this drive. He didn't respond to that. He held his sleeve against the little cut on his cheek that was bleeding a lot more than its size would indicate it could. One of my rings sliced him when I punched him. Good.

So, I drove and he talked. He apologized again about not telling me he was a cop. He confirmed what I had already figured out. He had sworn Luis and Brad to secrecy, until he could tell me "at the right time." I guffawed at that.

There wasn't a lot of traffic on Highway 101 midday on a Thursday, so speeding was easy. I was going eighty-five before I finally listened to Mickey and slowed down. He was right—the last thing I needed was to meet another cop.

Mickey was recapping where things stood. While part of me didn't want to listen to Mickey the Liar anymore, it was kind of helpful.

Mary: disappeared in Vegas and had two fake cops looking for her. She was probably a bad guy.

Jake: bad guy cop in Vegas, looking for me. Knew I was there with Mickey. Was going to take us where? Or anywhere?

Luis: good guy, helping out in Vegas somehow.

Cassie: murdered. By Georgia?

Georgia: could be connected to Jake, so probably a bad guy.

Nana: knew Mary, and at least had met Georgia. Murdered?

Hatpin: somebody stuck it in Nana's glasses case. Mickey paused. "Then there's the rapist guy that might be holding a grudge. Jerry Walbon."

I sped up again, gripping the steering wheel.

He touched my shoulder. "Slow down, Annabelle." I did.

I punched the radio on. We were far enough north to get reception for my favorite station, the Krush. They play new rock, old rock, singer-songwriters, unusual stuff, well-known stuff. Always mix it up. And right then the Subdudes were on—"You'll Be Satisfied," one of my most favorite songs in the world. Good music relaxes me, so I turned up the volume. Mickey started tapping his hand against his knee, while he was looking out the side of the car. I started singing along. And then, goddammit, he joined in.

I whipped my head around toward him. "The SUBDUDES? You know the SUBDUDES?"

"Annabelle! Drive the car! Watch the road!" I did turn back, but I was flustered. "MICKEY!"

"Shit, yes, they're my favorite band. What's your problem?"

I was in the lane second from the right, and after checking behind me, I swerved over to the far right, pulled up on the shoulder of the road, and came to a stop. I put the car in park and engaged the emergency brake, so I could turn and face him.

"Annabelle! For chrissakes! This is not smart at all. We could get hit sitting here!"

I just stared at him agape. "The SUBDUDES??? Aren't you from New York City? Are you telling me they played there? They are so NOT a New York City band!"

"I happen to have eclectic tastes, and yes, actually, they played at a little club on the Lower East Side several years ago, and I went to see them, and I now have all of their albums, and I sure hope that's okay with you! Jesus!"

I was speechless. My favorite band, his favorite band. He didn't like Andie McDowell. He was gorgeous. He was great in bed. He didn't seem to mind my ears. He told me that he was in love with me. This was all tooooo much.

"Tommy Malone…" I started.

"Unbelievably great guitar player, soulful singer. Johnny Magiore or whatever his name is on accordion and keyboards. And whatshisface on percussion, using mostly a tambourine and a mallet. Okay? You believe me?"

I nodded. "Steve Amadée. He's the percussionist. But they broke up."

"I know. Too bad for us." He paused. "All right, now, be careful pulling back out onto the freeway." He turned to look out behind us at the oncoming traffic. I didn't move. "Annabelle?"

I looked straight ahead and started to cry. Lots of tears, snot starting to run out of my nose. "Kleenex in my purse," I mumbled, and Mickey dug it out for me. I gave a hearty blow, and calmed down after a few moments.

"You okay?" he asked. He stroked my arm lightly. I let him.

"Wow, Mickey. I'm so far from okay it's ridiculous. And here you are, just about perfect in every way. But you lied to me, this huge, huge, ginormous lie, and I really want to love you, I do, and I want to trust you, I mean, we both love Tommy Malone? Are you kidding me?" I blew my nose again.

Mickey was patting my knee now. "It's going to work out. I don't know how, but it is. And I'll prove that you can trust me. I will. I promise." He looked behind us again. "Do you want me to drive?"

I released the emergency brake and put the car into gear. "No," I said. "I want you to be quiet." I floored it onto the highway, some dust kicked up behind us. I couldn't help but think of Steve McQueen in *Bullitt,* even though his Mustang was a green fastback.

Chapter Twenty

Tall Oaks is tucked into a residential neighborhood of Santa Rosa. Four one-story buildings are connected by walkways and halfway-decent landscaping. I can't say it's exactly feng-shui-ish, but it's pleasant. I parked in the visitors' lot. Mickey followed me into the main building. We hadn't talked for the rest of the drive. I had turned the radio back off, too, not wanting to know anything more about Mickey's musical tastes…not wanting to know anything more about Mickey, actually.

At the lobby entrance, I saw Martha Davis, one of the administrators, behind the welcoming desk. We smiled at each other. "Bea! How are you, sweetie?" She stood up and came to greet me with a warm hug.

I stiffened. Bea. I had forgotten that Martha always called me that. Mickey raised his eyebrows at me and said, "Bea?"

I raised my eyebrows back at him and returned Martha's hug. "Good to see you, too. Meet Mickey Paxton. Be careful what you say. He's official po-leece."

Mickey ignored me and shook her hand. "Martha."

She smiled at him and then moved back a step from both of us. "Mary Rosen?"

I jerked in response. "How in the world did you know that?"

"Sergeant Franklin of the San Francisco police called and told me to expect you. Let's sit down in the office and I'll tell you what I know."

She knew quite a bit. Mary had been missing since Monday. Martha had called her son to let him know. "We were especially worried because she hasn't been that steady on her feet, ever since she broke her foot."

So Mary hadn't lied about her broken foot, anyway. "She was in rehab for a while, right? Bad break? She fell?"

"Yes, in fact she was in your grandmother's room when she fell. You remember, she used to visit the Alzheimer's wing, and Nana was one of her favorites. She had climbed up on a chair…" Martha paused. "She said she was getting something down for Nana, but the only things up there were that old clock and a framed picture, I think, so that excuse never made any sense to me. I suppose Nana could have asked to see the picture, but she was ill at that point.…

Anyway, Mary fell and was in rehab for many weeks. She got back here not that long ago."

"Nana died while she was away."

"Yes, that's right."

"So, when you realized Mary was missing and you called her son, what did he say?" Mickey asked.

"He figured she had gone on another one of her gambling sprees and told me he'd start looking for her in Las Vegas."

I leaned forward. "Does her son live in Las Vegas?"

"Yes, indeed. He's a policeman, a detective, I think. A bit rough around the edges, but a solid individual. Treats his mother like a queen."

I grabbed Mickey's hand and squeezed it.

Mickey gave me a quick nod and then asked Martha, "What about Georgia Browning? Has she been here today, or yesterday evening?"

Martha looked confused. "Georgia? Why, no, she hasn't been here for a few weeks. She has done pro bono work for us, making sure that our residents and their families have their affairs in order, from wills to end-of-life preferences. But she had signed on to help us for six months, and that term finished, like I said, oh, around a month or two ago." Martha turned to me. "What does Georgia have to do with this?"

I shook my head. "We're not sure." I reached into my purse and pulled out the hatpin, careful not to stab myself, and showed it to her. "Ever seen this?"

Mary started. Her eyes got big. She squirmed in her chair. "Oh my goodness."

Mickey and I did a double-take. "What?!" we said in unison.

"That's Mary's hatpin." Martha took it from me and turned it over and over in her hands. "She used to wear it now and then. You might remember, Bea, that Mary is a great lover of very stylish hats?"

"Yes."

"Well, I asked her a few days before she broke her foot what had happened to the hatpin, because I hadn't seen her wearing it. She was vague about it and said that maybe she lost it. I thought she would have been devastated…"

Mickey interrupted again. "Devastated? Why? I mean, it is *just* a hatpin. It's pretty, and all that, but why would you think it was so important to her?"

Martha gazed at the pin and then looked up at Mickey. "Ah, Mr. Paxton, this is no simple hatpin. When Georgia was helping the residents here, she suggested that they have their jewelry appraised, so that after they die, their families would know the worth of individual pieces. Mary had this appraised. It's worth about $100,000."

"Jeez!" I jumped in my chair.

Martha nodded. "That's why I thought it was odd, when I asked her if she wanted to report it missing, that she shook her head and walked away from me." She paused. "I have to ask, how is it that *you* have the hatpin?"

"It was with Nana's things."

"Nana? Nana took it?"

I stood up. "Hey! No! You know better than that, Martha! I don't know how it got there!"

Martha stood up, too, and reached a hand out to me. "Dear, I don't mean any insult to Nana. It's just that Alzheimer's patients often don't know what's theirs and what isn't, and they take things, but it's not really stealing. It's part of their confusion." She patted my arm. We both sat back down.

Mickey took the hatpin from Martha. "So, it's worth a lot because of the one diamond? The diamond isn't that big, is it?"

Martha shook her head. "Well, actually, it's a good-sized diamond. Probably a carat. It could be worth a few thousand dollars, I would think." She folded her hands on her desk. "But apparently the pin is valued so highly because of who it used to belong to." We waited while she paused for effect. Martha had always had a flair for the dramatic. "No guesses, eh?"

"Martha, please," I said.

"Look on the back of it again, closely. Do you see any initials?"

Mickey and I examined it together. "Just 'Tarcelloni' and a zigzag line."

"Mm." She said. "Turn it around so that the line reads the other way."

Mickey did, and then showed it to me. MM. I gasped, "Marilyn MonROE??" at the same time that Mickey said, "Mike MEYers?" We looked at each other. "Mike Meyers? Are you crazy?"

Martha's smile was positively angelic. "That's what Mary told me."

We shook our heads. "What? What did she tell you?"

"That this belonged to Marilyn Monroe. That Joe DiMaggio bought it for her. And that Mary got it from an estate sale. She did some research and found a picture of Marilyn wearing a white hat and this pin was stuck in it."

"Did she show you the picture?" Mickey asked.

"No. But like I said, Georgia was the one who had it appraised for her, and that's the figure I remember. One hundred thousand smackeroos." Martha settled back in her chair and folded her arms, very satisfied with the sound of that last word sailing out of her mouth.

Mickey handed me the hatpin, pulled a notebook out of his sport coat pocket, and flipped it open. A pen from his inside front pocket followed.

I stared at him. "You have a notebook? You're going to take cop notes?"

He ignored me again, focusing on Martha. "When did you say that you noticed the pin was missing?"

Martha scrolled through her memory banks, eyes closed. "Shortly before your Nana died, Bea. We had a staff meeting to review patient care. I remember coming out into the hallway after that meeting and seeing Mary talking with Georgia and wearing her hat, sans pin." She preened, enjoying the sound of "sans" as much as "smackeroos."

Mickey snapped his notebook shut. "She was in Nana's room when she broke her foot. Maybe she had left the pin in there and was looking for it. "

I chewed the inside of my right cheek. "We need to talk to Georgia Browning again. We need to verify the story behind this pin. And we need to know where Jake is." I put the pin in my pocket.

"Do you mean Mary's son?" Martha pointed. "He's over in the common area, having some coffee."

Chapter Twenty-one

Remembering that moment, I realize that this was it, when it all fell together for me. Not what was going on—that was still going to take a little time. No, but who Mickey Paxton really was. Is. Whatever.

When we looked at each other after hearing that Jake was in the next room, it only took two seconds for me to jump up and say, "Let's go," while it took Mickey two seconds to jump up at the same time and say, "You stay here. I'll take a look."

Usually I wouldn't go for that. I'd say, what the hell, mister, I've got every right to confront this guy and don't treat me like your little lady, you overblown piece of macho hoo-ha.

But it hit me all at once. I mean, three things hit me all at once. Two came from looking into those endless eyes of his. I could read them, and they said, one, I'm a cop, and I know how to handle this, and two, I don't want you to get hurt. I knew right then that Mickey really did care about me. The third thing I realized was that I actually did not want to go see Jake. I was afraid, and I was tired of not knowing what was going on and people getting killed and my life getting trashed. So I sat back down, which surprised Mickey a little. He hesitated before turning and walking down the hall, waiting, I think, for an outburst from me. But then he left, his hand moving around to the inside of his jacket. Jeez, I thought, is he packing? And is that even the right word?

Martha scrutinized me. "You don't look so good."

I bit my lip. "Yeah, it's been a very long, weird, scary, surreal few days." I took a deep breath and let it out. "Tell me, Martha, what does Jake look like?" I was holding on to the ridiculously slight hope that Bad Goombah Cop Jake maybe wasn't the same Jake as Mary Rosen's son.

"Big man, kind of reminds me of Hoss Cartwright from *Bonanza,* though he talks like he's from New Jersey. I've always had a preference for big men. Not very attractive, to tell you the truth, but like I said, he's a good son." She suddenly leaned forward and tapped her finger on her desk. "I just remembered something. Georgia helped Jake get Mary into Tall Oaks. Another woman—very wealthy—had prepaid but didn't want to move in for several months, so Georgia suggested to the administration that they offer it at a reduced price to Mary in the interim. That way Jake could keep tabs on her until he could find her a permanent residence. I guess Georgia knew Jake from when she worked in Las Vegas."

I coughed. "Shit."

Then Mickey was back. He didn't look so hot, either.

"It's him, Annabelle. The big asshole. He didn't see me. I'm calling Brad. We'll get police here." He started punching in the number, talking to Martha at the same time. "How long did Jake say he would be staying?"

"He wanted a cup of coffee while he figured out what to do next. She put her finger to her lips, thinking. "He said something else, a bit strange though."

We both waited, watching her trace the outline of her lips. I never understand people who stop in the middle of telling you something, forcing you to say, "Yes?" or "And?" or "Oh, really, well why don't you hold that thought and tell us about it some other time. We'll call you tomorrow." So I did a palms-up shrug with my shoulders, giving her my best JUST TELL US look.

"He said that he was sure she would have *gotten back* by now, and when I said, oh, so you know where she's been? He mumbled something like, no not really, just figured she'd be here."

"He saw her in Las Vegas, Martha, and he and Mary might have been in touch since Mary ditched us." Mickey dropped his chin and talked into his phone, asking Brad for some Santa Rosa police backup. Then he hung up and gave Martha instructions. "I'd like you to get the other people in the common area out of there. Can you think of a way to do this, that won't make Jake suspicious?"

"I can try, but I'm not sure what this is all about. You're scaring me. It's just Jake, after all."

I would have spit out my coffee if I had been drinking any, but I wasn't, so I blew out some weird burble noise with my lips, like a horse. "*Just* Jake? He could have killed Mickey, and he kidnapped me at gunpoint."

Martha brought her hand again to her mouth. "Jake? Really? I thought he was a policeman!"

We answered in unison. "He is." Like that explained everything. She shook her head, and we stared without blinking back at her. Then she stood up.

"I'll get the others out of there and make sure they go back to their rooms, but really, I don't see the point of any of this. Jake's a nice man." She smoothed her hair.

Mickey thanked her as she left us, then sat down. I told him about the Geogia-Jake-Mary connection. He reached for my knee, and I let him land his hand there. "We're getting close, Annabelle. You okay?"

"Not really. I'm a little shaky. Too much going on. I don't want to see Jake again. It freaks me out, knowing he's been here when Nana was here. Knowing he could have hurt her."

"Why don't you go wait in the car?"

"Not gonna happen. You might need me." I flexed my right bicep and smiled. "I helped capture the bastard last time, remember?"

Mickey smiled back. "Dental floss. Got any on ya' this time?"

"No. But are you packing?"

Mickey let out a little laugh. "You mean, is that a gun in my pocket or am I glad to see you?"

I laughed a little, too. "Yeah."

"Both."

"You didn't have it on you in Las Vegas. How…?"

"Jake or whoever raided our suite tossed it aside and left it. I found it before you could. I hid it and then put it in my suitcase when you weren't looking, before we left for the airport."

"What is it?"

"A nine millimeter Glock. Seventeen rounds."

"Wow."

He kissed me softly. "The police will be here any minute. Then we'll figure out what the hell is going on."

"Okay." I kissed him gently, too. "You know what you said before, in Gumps?"

"You mean when you socked me in the nose?"

"Hey, I pretty much missed your nose, but…"

"Yes, I remember that vividly. It was only about ninety minutes ago, as I recall."

"You meant it?"

Mickey nodded. "I'm in deep, Beatrice Annabelle, and I've not handled it well. But you've swept me away. Absolutely."

I sighed. "I could have been a broom."

He studied my face, holding my hands, our knees touching. "I am completely in love with you."

Jake exploded into the room. He leaped toward Mickey and punched him over in his chair, landing on top of him. I fell backward, too, and got up to see Jake pummeling Mickey in the face. I screamed and jumped on Jake and beat him with my fists and scratched and even bit at him, wherever I could and however fast I could, but it didn't seem to be making much of a difference.

When I realized that Mickey was trying to roll away from Jake, and I wasn't helping by being on top of both of them, I hopped onto my feet. I screamed some more while I kicked Jake and fumbled for the hatpin in my pocket. I finally grabbed it like a dagger and lunged, sticking it deep into his neck. I'd never stuck anything into anyone before, but somehow I managed it.

I jumped back, while Jake growled and rolled off of Mickey, twisting to pull the pin out of his neck.

Mickey scrambled to his feet and got his gun out of his shoulder holster, but his face was really bloody and he was staggering around. I hurriedly wrapped my arms around him from the back to steady him so that he could aim at Jake. I clearly missed Jake's carotid artery, because no massive jet of blood spurted from his neck, but blood was oozing out, and he was pissed. He swung toward us, on his feet now, and charged.

I called, "Halt! Police!" because Mickey hadn't pulled himself together yet. But Mickey knew Jake was coming toward us, and he clicked his Glock, which meant he was ready to shoot. I know this from far too many cop movies.

Jake stopped. "Who the fuck do ya' think ya' fuckin' are, ya fuckin' fuckheads?"

Mickey still wasn't talking, so I spit out, "We're the fucking po-fucking-leece, you fucking moron, so get down on your fucking knees and put your fucking hands behind your fucking head. Right now, you creepy fuck." Sometimes in conversation I follow the lead of others.

Mickey began weaving, like he was losing his balance, so I braced myself behind him, let him lean against me, my arms now straight out in front alongside his, which were still holding the already clicked gun. I kept talking. "This gun is fucking already clicked, in case you didn't fucking hear that, Mr. Fuck."

"Clicked? CLICKED? What the fuck." He launched himself at us again.

Mickey was ready to shoot him. I was frightened to my core that various scenarios would play out, like he would miss and hit the wall behind Jake, which was probably the wall to some sweet old man's bedroom, and we'd end up killing the poor old man, and Mickey would fall down dead from loss of blood, and I would be strangled by Jake while I was trying to figure out how to reclick the Glock.

But none of that happened. A heavy voice from behind us ordered, "Drop it. Now. All of you. Down on the floor, slowly, face down, hands over your heads."

Three guys in uniform came in, guns drawn on Mickey and me and Jake. Jake put his arms up in the air and said, "I'm police, Vegas."

"Get down on the floor now. We'll get IDs in a minute."

Mickey let his arms drop and fell to his knees. I managed to kneel down next to him, then we both were on the floor, and one of the new cops had taken his gun. Mickey said, "I'm Detective Paxton. I'm the one who called Brad Franklin and asked for you guys to get here. ID is in my pocket."

Handcuffs came out and I was relieved, figuring Jake was being restrained. Then I felt my own hands being pulled behind my back and shoved into cuffs. "Hey! What are you doing?" I squirmed.

"Don't tell me," the guy said, "you're a police officer, too?"

"No! But I'm…" I didn't know how to explain who I was in short order. "I'm this guy's girlfriend. And he's a good cop. And that guy over there, he's a bad cop."

"Thanks for the recap, sister. We're all going to get up now and sit down, and I'll figure out who's who."

I was pulled to my feet, as were Mickey and Jake, and they shepherded us into lobby chairs.

It only took a few minutes for them to check the IDs, confer with Brad on their phone, take the cuffs off of me and Mickey, and haul Jake off to the police station, where Brad would meet them to help with the questioning. They called an ambulance for Mickey, even though he said I could drive him to the hospital. I was still shaky, so I insisted on the ambulance. It arrived quickly. I sat in the back with him while the EMT mopped his face and checked his blood pressure. I got to sit there and hold his hand, because, as I explained to the EMT, I was his girlfriend.

"I'm his girlfriend."

"Yes, I know, third time you've told me that."

Mickey smiled.

And that's when I realized that the last time I saw the hatpin was when Jake pulled it out of his neck.

Chapter Twenty-two

Mickey's eye was not in good shape. He had a detached retina. This meant that he needed surgery soon, or he could go permanently blind in that eye. As it was, his vision was really blurry. He was wearing an eye patch in order to see clearly out of the good eye. I told him it looked sexy—he had a bit of a Johnny-Depp-in-*Pirates of the Caribbean* thing going on—but either he didn't believe me or he didn't care. He was also really sore. Getting beat up by Jumbo Jake can do that to you. Every time he moved he let out a little groan. There was a lot of groaning going on as we left the hospital to take a cab back to the Mustang.

Brad had called Mickey's cell phone and left a message while we were in the hospital. Mickey picked it up in the back seat of the cab. He listened, and then disconnected. "Fuck."

"Fuck?"

He looked out the window. I didn't like it that he wasn't looking at me, his girlfriend.

"Mickey, fuck?" I touched his arm.

He turned back to me. "They let him go."

"WHAT?" Mickey winced a bit—I guess his eardrums were sore, too—and the cab driver swerved and gave me a dirty look in the rear-view mirror. "HOW could they have DONE that?"

"They have nothing on him except our fight, and he said he didn't start it. He also swore he never saw us in Las Vegas, and he had an alibi that checked out."

"What."

"Doesn't matter what. The guy's a police officer. And your pal Martha was no help. Said she didn't know a thing except that your grandmother might have stolen Mary's hatpin and that Jake is a good son." Mickey went back to looking out the window.

All of this was turning out to be my fault, though I really didn't know how. I was miffed about the "your pal" comment, but I was trying to be super nice since Mickey was in pain. I sank back in the seat. We didn't speak for the rest of the cab ride.

I paid the driver, who didn't appreciate my generous tip, and Mickey slid into the Mustang's passenger seat, leaving me to drive. I almost reminded him that I wasn't on the rental car contract, but he wouldn't have found that amusing.

Once we were buckled in, I said, "Jake has the hatpin." Mickey brought his hand to his forehead and sighed. I added, "Martha is not my goddamn pal." Then I turned the key in the ignition, and we headed back to the Sheraton Palace Hotel.

Mickey ran a bath and got in. I lay face down on the bed and tried to breathe deeply to calm myself, then realized I could barely breathe at all, since I was face down in the pillow. I turned over onto my back, stared at the ceiling, and dozed off for a few minutes.

When I woke up, I walked into the bathroom and found Mickey in the tub, his eyes closed. I felt the water. It was starting to cool, so I touched his shoulder gently.

"I'm not asleep." Then he opened his eyes.

"The water's getting cold. You should get out."

Once he was standing I wrapped a towel around him. "Lean on me while you step out of the tub. I don't want you to slip."

He put his arm around me and as he lifted one foot out, his other slipped, and he fell into me. I lost my balance, landing both of us on the floor. "Oh, god, Mickey, I'm sorry, here, let me help you up." I scrambled to my feet and then squatted down to try to help him sit up, my hands holding him under his armpits. He was sitting, leaning against the toilet. "Come on, we can do this."

"Let go." I did, and I sat down on the toilet. After a moment of drying himself, sitting on the floor, he patted the tiles. "Come here."

I slid off the toilet and sat down next to him. He dropped his towel around his neck. "There's something you don't know."

"Those are five words I don't want to hear at this moment."

He sighed. "Are you ready?"

"I guess I have to be. Go ahead. What is it? You're married? You're not really a cop, you're a gangster? You're actually gay? You don't live in New York? You hate the Subdudes? You've been investigating me? You think I'm a murderer? You don't…"

Mickey put his hand gently over my mouth and looked me in the eyes. "I think Brad is involved."

I went silent. I couldn't have said much anyway with his hand over my mouth.

He took his hand away. "You were right. It was too coincidental that he showed up on this case. And he let Jake go much too quickly. I think these bad cops have some sort of multi-city network."

I liked it that he thought I was right. I didn't like it that bad cops seemed to be sprouting up all over the place like a wicked case of acne.

"There's something else you don't know."

I was sure I didn't want to hear this either.

"Okay."

"Listen to me very carefully, Annabelle."

"I am. Just tell me." He was scaring me.

"I'm crazy ass in love with you. And I don't want to go anywhere ever again without you."

Apparently I had been holding my breath, because a huge exhale poured out of me at those words, and I started crying, yet again. "You don't really know me, Mickey, and I've caused you all this trouble. I can't see how you love me, I really can't," I sputtered. "You're going to realize when this is over that you're not that interested in me, so please don't say that you love me because then when you leave it will just make it worse."

He took my face in his hands and kissed my forehead, each cheek, and my nose, which was running rather terribly. "To tell you the truth, you've taken me completely by surprise. But here we are on the bathroom floor, a one-eyed beat-up cop and a confused, enchanting publicity manager, and I can't move without hurting, and you can't stop crying, and I can't imagine being anywhere else right now."

I hugged him until I stopped crying. I dried my face on his towel and sat up. "Food. We'll think better with food. I'll order room service. And then I'll check in with Mom and Dad. What do you want to eat?"

"French fries. Red wine. A bottle. The most expensive pinot on the wine list. And ice cream. Chocolate."

I grinned. "You gotta be kidding me."

He grinned, wincing. "Not at all. That's what I want."

"And here I was thinking you couldn't get more perfect. Do you want help standing up?"

Mickey was already pushing himself up from the floor. "No, I got it."

From the bedroom I dialed room service, ordering double of everything Mickey said, including the bottle of wine. Then I picked up my cell phone and dialed my parents' house. I had already checked in with them from the hospital and told them everything that had happened. I wanted to hear their voices again. Mom answered, and I said, "Hi, it's me."

"Sweetheart, you must be completely exhausted. Why don't you and Mickey come here for the night? I'll get take-out from that Thai restaurant."

I rubbed my eyes. "Mickey can barely move, and we just ordered room service."

"Hmm. Well, I wonder, are you out of danger now, since that Jake fellow got the hatpin?."

"Good question. If he and Mary were after us for the hatpin, and now they have it, maybe this nightmare is over. The only thing left to do is to figure out how it all happened in the first place. Like, what is Georgia's part in all of this? And"—my eyes filled up with tears—"Cassie, what about Cassie? I mean, is that hatpin really worth a life? We still don't know about Nana, either." Tears burned my face.

"Oh, honey. Take a nice, hot bath and get some sleep." She lowered her voice. "I don't like it that they let Jake go. I mean, he pummeled the shit out of Mickey, after all."

"How do you know that they let Jake go?"

"Just a minute, Bea. In that cupboard, to the right, Brad. Now, honey, what did you ask? Oh, right, well Brad told us, we're about to sit down with him…"

I choked and coughed and sat up straight. "Brad?"

"Yes. Got here a few minutes ago. He came to ask some more questions about Nana. The three of us were sitting down for a drink. You must be very careful, darling, until we've figured this all out."

"MOM!"

"What is it, sweetheart?"

My whole body ached. "MOM! Where is Brad, right now?"

Mickey came out of the bathroom at that moment, and we locked eyes.

"Honey, he's right here, in the kitchen with me. I'm just pouring him a Scotch. What on earth is the matter? Brad is…"

I got as much control over my voice as I could muster. "Mom. Listen to me. You have to figure out a way to get him out of the house. Do you hear me? Don't let him hear this conversation because…"

A new voice came on the phone. "Annabelle, hi, it's Brad. Your mother and father are very hospitable. Where are you?… Yes, Mrs. Starkey, that will be great. Just a splash of soda…" I could hear Mom tell him to for chrissakes just call her Sylvia. "Anyway, is Mickey all right? And why in the world do you want me out of the house?" This last question was posed with a quieter voice, one that I did not like one little bit.

"Brad." That was all I could manage. I was still staring at Mickey. He quickly grabbed the pad and pen by the phone, scribbled something and handed it to me. "Mickey's fine." I was reading his notes. "He's not with me at the moment. I'm at the apartment. Mickey had to run some…"—Mickey's handwriting was not the clearest I had ever seen— "…errands," I stammered.

Brad paused. I heard him take a sip. How dare he drink my parents' good Scotch. "You didn't answer my question. Why do you want me out of here?" He was whispering.

"Why do I want you out of my parents' house?" I repeated, for Mickey's sake, hoping he'd provide the next line of dialogue. Unfortunately, he was concentrating on pulling on his boxers.

"That's the question, Annabelle. I'm here for a friendly chat. Jake visited Martha after I had him released, and he found out from her where your parents live. Said there might be something here that could clear up your lesbian friend's murder." He sipped again.

"CASSIE! HER NAME WAS CASSIE!" I yelled, and Mickey jumped, wide-eyed, and vigorously shook his head no no no, like, don't let on that you're scared or pissed or ANYTHING. I took a breath and continued in what I hoped was a calm voice. "I don't want my parents involved. They have nothing to do with any of this. I want you to leave them alone. Please put my mother back on."

"Aaah. Well, I'd give the phone back to Sylvia, but she's in the den now with Jeff, where I'll be joining them. I'll let her know that you're fine. I suggest that you make your way here as soon as possible. And bring Mickey with you, wherever he is. I won't be leaving any time soon." And with that, he hung up.

I dropped the phone, trembling. "Mickey."

Mickey was halfway dressed. "I know. Let's get out of here and to your parents." He eased himself onto the desk chair and put on his shoes. "On the way we'll call Luis and my partner in New York—I filled him in yesterday. We need to find some law enforcement in this whole charade that we can trust."

I hadn't moved. "What if Jake is on his way there?"

Mickey stopped tying his shoes. "I don't know why he would be, but hell, what do I know. Brad is enough to worry about right now."

He slowly stood up and pulled a t-shirt over his head, then managed to position his shoulder holster. He gingerly slipped into his sport coat. "Let's go, Annabelle."

I still couldn't move.

"I can't leave you here. Jake could be on his way to your apartment, or to this room, to find either or both of us. We need to stick together." He adjusted his eye patch. "Stand up. Grab your purse. Pick up your phone. Put on your jacket. Now."

I did all of those things. At the door we heard a knock and "Room service!" We opened the door. Mickey grabbed the check and signed it. I grabbed the two plates of French fries and told the waiter to keep the ice cream and to leave the wine in the room. I set the plates down on the bed while Mickey made his way down the hall. I grabbed a pillow and shook it out of the pillowcase. I dumped the French fries in the pillowcase. The waiter watched me, amused.

"We're in a hurry. Thanks." I followed Mickey down the hall in a quick trot, the sack of fries slung over my shoulder like Santa Claus' bag of gifts.

Chapter Twenty-three

On the way to Palo Alto, in between mouthfuls of French fries, Mickey called New York and then Luis. I was driving. Luis said he'd check with some guys in Las Vegas, to see if they could alert some reputable cops for us. He also told Mickey that he had a face-to-face with his captain, and as a result, they started a full-fledged investigation into Jake. Already they had connected him with two gangsters—Luis' word, not mine—and a casino robbery. Luis identified the two fake cops who stopped us in the parking lot from photos taken at that robbery, photos that Jake had stashed away at the bottom of an evidence box.

That wasn't all.

Luis confirmed that Georgia had been the legal consultant at one of the casinos where Jake handled security. She had no previous experience as an estate lawyer.

"She's a phony, Mickey, besides being pals with Jake," I mumbled through a mouthful of French fries.

"Looks that way. She's definitely in this, whatever *this* is."

I tried to concentrate on the road while my mind was racing. What if Jake and his friends were in California now, looking for Mary and us? We still didn't know why. I did know that Brad was bad, and I couldn't bear to think of Mom and Dad beaten up or worse—each time I did, I got the shakes. Instead I tried to come up with some answers to explain this mind-boggling horror show.

What I couldn't figure was why these guys were still interested in us, or my parents. Jake had the hundred thousand dollar hatpin. What did they want? What did I, or Mickey, or my parents have to do with anything? Did they think all along that I had the pin, and that's why Cassie got killed? Or was it something else entirely involving Georgia Browning, that had nothing to do with the hatpin?

I was driving too fast again, but this time, Mickey didn't say a word. He kept handing me fries while he was talking on the phone. His partner promised to see who he could find in the SFPD. Mickey gave him my parents' address.

When we got to their neighborhood—dotted with freshly painted houses accented by manicured lawns and spotless luxury coupes—the contrast of its movie-set perfection to what I imagined was going on inside my family home almost made me laugh.

Mickey had me pull over on the street a few houses before Mom and Dad's and turn the ignition off. I rubbed my salty, greasy hands against my black capris and we both got out of the car, quietly shutting the doors. It was good to be dressed in all black. A brief image of Uma Thurman in *Kill Bill* crossed my mind, even though I look like her as much as I look like Halle Berry.

There was a black sedan in the driveway—we figured it was Brad's. We didn't see any other cars. The outside lights were on. Nothing seemed out of the ordinary. I guess it's often true that nothing *seems* out of the ordinary when in fact, nothing is the least bit ordinary.

At the front door, I had my key out when the door opened. Brad grinned a welcome. "Come on in, kids. We've been expecting you." He pointed his gun at us. "And, you should give me your gun, Mick." He held out his hand. "Nice patch, by the way."

Mickey pulled his gun out and handed it over. "What are you doing, Brad? This isn't smart. Why don't we…"

Brad put Mickey's Glock in his pocket. "Why don't you shut up and come inside. I'm wrapping up a case here, and I can come up with reasons for arresting the whole lot of you.

Go into the den there with Sylvia and Jeff, and we'll all have a nice, long talk." I hated hearing my parents' names sliming out of his mouth. I ground my teeth.

We walked into the den. Mom and Dad were sitting very calmly on the couch, but their rigid faces showed that they were anything but calm. When I saw Dad mopping blood with his handkerchief from a big welt on his forehead, I gasped. He held up his hand to stop me. "I'm all right, Bea, I'm all right."

"Yeah, he's all right," Brad said. "Let's hope he's learned not to try any more heroics."

"Dad, what...?"

Mom was holding onto Dad's arm. "Honey, perhaps you and Mickey should just sit down."

"Now, that's a good idea." Brad motioned me with his head to the other side of Mom, and Mickey to one of two recliners. Brad took the other. "Isn't this cozy?"

"What do you want, Brad?" Mickey clenching his jaw reminded me of Harrison Ford in *Air Force One,* which wasn't a very good movie, but who can resist Harrison Ford?

"Jake has the hatpin, Brad," I added, "if that's what you're looking for."

I could tell that this was not news to Brad. "Mmm hmm. I know. He told me."

"So what do you want?" Mickey's jaw was still clenched. "You're holding a gun on us, which hardly seems necessary."

Brad took a sip of Scotch. "I want the other hatpin."

"WHAT other hatpin?" I shouted.

Mom answered. Her jaw was clenched, too, and she sounded a bit like Cherry Jones playing the president on *24,* telling some-one or other to find Jack Bauer. "Mr. Franklin here has been telling us all about the other *fucking* hatpin. It has to do with a certain clock." She was staring at Brad, who was staring at me.

I looked at Mom. "A clock? Huh?"

She turned to me. "Mister Fucking Franklin says that there are two hatpins, and that Mary Rosen hid the other one in an old clock."

I frowned at Mom, then at Mickey, then at Brad. But before I could speak—because I was ready to tell Brad to go upstairs to Mom's office and get the old clock and shake it around and if a hatpin fell out he could have it, if we could all please just *live*—Brad said, "I did search the house for a clock, took your parents with me on my little tour." He waved his gun at them. "That's when Daddy Jeff grabbed a vase upstairs and threw it at me." He paused. "Anyway, the only clocks I found were the one on the wall in the kitchen," he nodded toward it, "an alarm clock in one bedroom, and a digital clock in another bedroom."

I cast a puzzled frown toward Mom. She shook her head ever so slightly. How could Brad have not found Nana's clock? Had Mom hidden it somehow? Why would she *do* that? Were we really going to die for a clock that hadn't worked in at least thirty years?

Mickey probed Brad. "Exactly what are we all doing here? There's no clock, there's no second hatpin, you've hurt Jeff, he'll probably need stitches, you're waving your gun like a wand, and I don't see how this can end well. Want to clue us in?"

Brad sneered. "I figure maybe she"— his gun waved at Mom—"has hidden that clock or that hatpin somewhere else in this house. Here's the thing: Jake will be showing up here in a little while with two, uh, associates, who are flying in from Vegas. Once they're here, we're going to tear this place apart. Then we'll decide what to do with all of you." He obviously enjoyed the thought.

"You're going to KILL us for a measly $100,000???!! Or is it $200,000 now?" I screamed. I'd had enough of this calm-demeanor shit.

Brad's contempt for me oozed from his cold, steely gaze. He pulled a cigarette out of his front pocket, stuck it in his mouth, and lit it. I didn't know that he smoked. I guess while he was playing Brad Franklin The Good Sergeant, he hid his habit. Now that he was Brad Franklin The Piece-of-Shit Cop, no more pretense. He took a drag and blew a long stream of smoke toward us. "I don't know where you got that $100,000 figure. They're worth a lot more than that."

"Well, the one I know about belonged to Marilyn Monroe! Joe DiMaggio bought it for her! It belongs in a museum!"

He snickered at that, eyeing me with derision. "Ah, yes, I heard that Martha Davis story, too, from the cops who busted all of you at Tall Oaks. It's a good one. But it's nonsense." He sucked on his cigarette, held his inhale, then blew out. "Those hatpins are much more than hatpins."

"What the hell are you talking about?"

Brad pointed his pistol at Mickey. "You got yourself a live one, there, Mick. But you might want to advise her to calm the fuck down." He shifted the aim of his gun to my face. "The hatpins are sharp on one end"—he fingered the trigger—"as Jake surely knows now! But the other ends, with the enamel and gold? They actually spring open and voilá, each holds a key, to a double-lock strong box. Where there's a ton of dough. A helluva lot more than one hundred thousand K."

Dad spoke up. "Where is this strong box? Why not just get it and blow it open?"

"It's in a bank. In a safe deposit box. Jake's got the key to that. But we need both hatpins to get what's inside. Now, no one wants all that money and jewelry blown up, or lost, especially after all the work Mary and Georgia did to put it there." Brad stubbed out his cigarette on the arm of the chair. He lit another, taking his time.

We were collectively holding our breath while he sucked in his. Then Mickey and I said at the same time, "Georgia Browning." Brad took a drag, savoring the moment. "There's a lot of money to be made off old folks. That was Georgia's racket, and she was good at it."

"You knew who Georgia Browning was all along." Mickey was disgusted.

"Yeah. When you two came to the station with your sad little story about finding her, I knew I couldn't protect her anymore."

I inhaled a sharp breath of smoky air. "You're saying Georgia killed Cassie and you were supposed to cover it up."

He took another drag and went back to waving his gun around. "Your lesbo friend was in the wrong place at the wrong time, surprised Georgia when she was searching your apartment. It was unfortunate. She didn't mean to kill her, but I guess she didn't know her own strength."

"You've been in on this all along." Mickey practically spat the words out.

"Jake and I go back a long ways. We were at the police academy together. But, no, I got in on this deal just a few days ago. I'm ready to hang up my badge—too many pissy rules about how we have to be nice to the scum we bust our asses to arrest."

I frowned. "What about Mary? Why was she in Las Vegas?"

"Looking for you. She figured you had at least one of the hatpins with you."

"WHY would she think THAT?"

He smiled, like he was on top of the world. "She broke her foot when she fell after hiding the second pin, Georgia's, in the clock."

I suddenly remembered the big hat that Georgia was wearing in the photograph taken at Tall Oaks.

Jake continued. "Mary had already stuck her pin in the glasses case. Lost her balance and fell. Then your granny kicked the bucket while Mary was in rehab. When she got out, Martha told her you packed up your granny's things. Said you mentioned something about maybe using the case."

The glasses case. I found it on Nana's bureau when I gathered up her things. Martha was watching me—she is really nosy—and maybe I did say something to her about that case.

"Why did Mary hide the pins? And why in Nana's glasses case and whatever clock you're talking about?"

"She had some sort of falling out with Georgia—something about Georgia running a separate scam on a rich widow. Mary got Georgia's key and booted her out of the deal, probably on threat of sicking Jake on her. But she knew Georgia was a risk and could put the whole plan in jeopardy. The worst place for her to hide the keys would be in her own room." He laughed. "That's why your little old Nana ended up an unknowing accomplice." He snorted. "Mary told Jake everything, and he, well, *insisted,* that Georgia find the glasses case in your apartment." He grinned.

Mickey leaned toward me. "Georgia broke into your apartment to find the glasses case, and she heard your message on the machine about going to Las Vegas…"

"…with a complete stranger named Mickey Paxton, and she told Mary to look for me there."

"And Mary told Jake, so they were both looking for you…"

"And it was no accident they were both on the elevator…"

"And she picked us up in Luis' cab, and…

"And she looked through my purse. Wow."

Brad shrugged. "Yeah. Wow. Got it in six." He exhaled through his nose, slowly. "Jake was none too pleased that his little old mother had lost the hatpins." He tapped ash on the braided rug. "Mary was afraid to face him after she didn't find the pin on you." He chuckled.

"Now what, Brad, are you going to kill us after you and your pals ransack the house?" I tried not to sound as frightened as I felt. *Stay cool, Annabelle, as cool as Lauren Bacall in* To Have and Have Not. *Just put your lips together and blow.*

Brad smirked. "Kill you? Have you forgotten that I'm the law? I won't have to kill you unless you resist arrest. See, once the pins are found, I can come up with enough, uh, *evidence,* to implicate you and your mommy and daddy as thieves. After I get the keys, I can make a case that you stole the hatpins, thinking they were valuable in themselves. Georgia will go down for the murder. I get her third of the payout. Jake and I will split for Rio, with or without Mother Mary, with our fortune from the strongbox. Now Mickey here, he might have to die assaulting an officer. I'm still working that part out, girlie."

Girlie!

I lunged for him then, or rather, I tried to, but Mom grabbed my waist and pulled me back down.

"Better not call her 'girlie' if you want to keep all your teeth," muttered Dad.

I sat seething, elbows on knees, head in my hands, trying to control my breathing. Looking at the floor, I wondered why Mom was wearing four-inch high heels. I shifted my gaze to the coffee table and noticed a business card lying face down. It was Brad's, the one I had given to Dad the day before. I stared at it, looked back at Mom's shoes, and felt my face flush. My body tingled from head to toe as everything fell into place. In that instant, I knew Georgia Browning hadn't killed Cassie and probably had never been in my apartment. I also knew it would be a miracle if we all got out of this alive.

Chapter Twenty-four

I took a deep breath and sat back up. "Okay, go ahead, search the house. You can have your lousy hatpins and your money and do whatever you want with it all. Let my parents go and just deal with me. And Mickey."

"Bea!" Mom and Dad sort of gasped my name at once.

Brad stubbed out this cigarette right on the wood coffee table. "Mickey, old pal, I have to admit, there's a lot of satisfaction in finding you mixed up in this. What a riot! Mary and Jake are looking for the broad who's fucking the self-righteous holier-than-thou Michael Paxton! How is she in the sack? Worth all of this?" He laughed.

Dad shot up. "You watch your mouth, you hear me?" Mom pulled him back down.

Brad kept talking, and his voice got even nastier. "You always thought you were better than me. Hell, my own wife thought you were better than me. So, fuck you, Paxton."

Mickey shifted in the recliner, to better confront Brad. "Patty clearly came to her senses. You are such a prick. You shoved her around once, when you were drunk, and she called me, hysterical. I told her to leave you then, but I guess she stuck it out a while longer. What did you finally do? Break her bones?"

Brad sprang to his feet and shoved his pistol against Mickey's forehead. Dusty sat up and growled. Mom screamed. Dad and I jumped up. Brad snarled at us. "Sit the fuck down, now." We did. Dusty stayed sitting up, alert.

Brad backed away from Mickey and sat back down, too. "Enough talk. Everyone shut up while we wait for Jake."

Mickey rubbed his forehead, and I instinctively started rubbing my own. "Hey, Brad. Did you kill my grandmother?" Dad twitched, Mom let out a little cry.

Brad snickered. "Hell, no. I'm the new guy on the team. I didn't kill the old lady, and neither did Jake or Mary or Georgia. They don't kill the old people; they just rob them. No need to kill the walking dead."

"You lousy fucking asshole dickhead creep."

"Ditto," my mother said.

He leered at her. Mom flipped him the bird.

"Now, Georgia killing Cassie Hobbs, well, like I said, that was a mistake. But she'll be found and convicted. More money for me."

I pounced on that comment like hungry black panther. "I doubt that, you dirtbag."

Brad chuckled. "What's that supposed to mean?"

"Georgia didn't kill Cassie. You did."

Mickey leaned his head back against the recliner and closed his eyes. His good eye, anyway, the other hidden behind his patch. He looked gray. Mom and Dad turned toward me with surprise.

Brad's thumb stroked his gun. "I just told you, idiot. Georgia killed her."

"No, *you* did. Georgia couldn't have. She's petite, and short. Remember, Mickey? She couldn't have bashed my door in. Not a chance."

Mickey rubbed his cheek. "She was tall, as I remember..."

"Shoes! Didn't you notice her shoes? She was wearing four-inch high heels with platforms, and she was about my height *with them on.* Plus she was slight, thin. She couldn't have killed Cassie."

Mickey frowned, maybe trying to recall Georgia's shoes.

Brad tapped his gun on his knee, probably ruminating on something very different from shoes, then raised his eyes to confront me. "If Georgia isn't the killer, what makes you think you can accuse me, you little bitch?"

I was starting to shake. I didn't know if it was a mistake to piss off Brad even more by showing my hand. He had a couple of guns on him, after all, and could blow us all away. But he could do that no matter what.

So I kept talking. "You went to my apartment to look for the glasses case. You wrote her name on my notepad. You've been lying to everyone about her, pretending that you don't know her. But once the police find out you were in my apartment *before* the investigation and wrote her name and number down, you'll be their number-one suspect."

Mickey sat up, alert. "How do you know?"

"The G and the B." I picked up Brad's business card and handed it to him. "See? Look on the back of his card, here, where he wrote her name and address in the interrogation room? They're the same as the G and the B on the notepad. I shoved the card into my pocket then and handed it to Dad last night. I never saw the back of it until just now."

Mickey studied it, with his good eye. "You're right."

Brad watched, shaking his head. "What are you, some kind of handwriting expert?"

"Anybody can tell this is the same handwriting. You know, at the police station when I told you about the notepad, I thought that you were just pissed off at me. Now I know you were pissed off at your own stupid self. Bonkers was already under my bed and on top of the notepad when the police—I mean police who aren't scumbag murderers—got there. They'll know you were in my apartment." My shaking was turning into all-over body shivering. "Pretty stupid, Brad, dropping that notepad."

Brad waved his gun at me. "You can't prove anything. You gave me the notepad, and I've already destroyed it."

Suddenly my trembling stopped. I leaned in, forearms on knees, and smiled. "Um, not all of it, asshole." I pointed my fingers at him, using Luis' gunslinger move.

Everyone froze. The vibe in the room shifted. It felt thick and heavy, stifling. I was sweating. Brad stopped playing with his gun and pointed it at my head. "What are you talking about?"

"I rubbed over the second sheet on the pad, too, and ripped it out. It's not as clear as the top sheet, but it's legible."

Mickey blinked his eye and started calculating. "When?"

"Before we went to visit Georgia. You were in the shower."

Brad got up and walked over to me. He raised the gun like he was going to hit me with it. "Where is it?"

I jumped at the gun, flinging myself onto Brad and clutching him as we crashed against the coffee table. Mickey was up in the next second. Brad fired. Mickey fell down. Mom screamed. Dad grabbed her head and they ducked. I fought free and crawled to Mickey, who was writhing in pain.

Brad yelled, "Stupid! Very stupid!"

That's when Dusty took over. Golden retrievers, as you probably know, are not known for their fierceness, but that gunshot brought out her inner rottweiler. She clamped Brad's leg in her jaws, biting down and growling. Dad joined the action, leaping up to grab a heavy brass table lamp and smash it on Brad. He got him on his ribcage and Brad went down. Mom yanked off her shoes to beat Brad with sharp whacks. He couldn't shield himself with Dusty doing her best to shred his leg into spaghetti. Mom was cursing like a maniac. Dad found the phone on the floor and dialed 9-1-1, leaving the line open and tossing the receiver onto the couch. He wrestled the gun from Brad, dodging Mom's blows, sat on him, pointing the gun at the back of his head, and screamed over to the phone, "Send police! Intruder! Gun shots! Police officer down!"

Brad bucked suddenly, trying to throw Dad off him. Dad dug his knees in, his legs straddling Brad. He whacked him on the head with the gun. Brad went still.

Mom stopped hitting Brad, out of breath. "We need to tie him up!" She darted around the room, wild-eyed.

I was on the floor next to Mickey. I had ripped off my shirt and was tying it around his leg, to stop the bleeding. "Over here, Mom! Mickey's shot!"

She stopped. "But what do we do about…"

Mickey quietly urged, "Handcuffs. Use his handcuffs." Mom sprang back into action, reaching around under Brad's jacket, finding handcuffs, and with Dad's help, rolling him over and clamping them, his arms jerked back hard. Dusty still worked on his leg. Dad stood up, gun still pointed at Brad. "Don't move, you lousy prick."

Mom rushed over to Mickey and carefully inspected the hole in his thigh while I held his hand. "It's clean, through and through. Annabelle, get me antiseptic, gauze, and tape from the medicine chest."

I ran to the upstairs bathroom and came back with the bandages along with a hand towel. I tossed the towel to Dad. "Gag him."

While Mom went to work on Mickey, Dad rolled the towel the long way and gagged Brad with it, tying its ends tight behind his head. Then he petted Dusty. "Good girl, that's all right now."

Dusty let go. She walked over to Mickey and licked his face, and then lay down beside him with her head resting on his chest, and we all waited for the good guys to show up.

Chapter Twenty-five

When we heard a car pull up in the driveway, a very few minutes later, Mom, still kneeling with me next to Mickey, putting pressure on his wound, snapped, "Well, it's about fucking time." I thought her a bit unfair. It seemed to me that the police had gotten there miraculously fast. Too fast, in fact. The doorbell rang, and Mom yelled, "Just come in! Now!" and cursed again, "Jesus fucking Christ." Dusty barked, but she stayed with Mickey.

Mickey yelled "No!" and lucky for us, the front door was locked. I jumped up and fastened the deadbolt and leaned my back against the door.

Mom looked at Mickey and then me, stunned. Dad put a foot on Brad's chest on the floor, his hands weary from holding that gun. I'd bet my entire collection of Nancy Drew mystery books that it was the first time he ever had a gun in his hand, let alone belted a murderer on the head with one. He took a deep breath. "It's not the police, Sylvia."

Mickey lifted his head just enough to meet my eyes. "Stall them, Annabelle, until the police get here." Then to Mom, "Sylvia, Jeff's right. These are not the police. That's Jake and his friends. Police could not have gotten here this fast. And they wouldn't be ringing the doorbell and waiting for us to answer it."

Brad grunted.

"Oh god." Mom looked at Dad, who was shaking now. I was afraid he would drop the gun.

I walked over to him. "Let me take over for a bit, Dad. Really, I'm getting good at this stuff." He hesitated but gave me the gun. I couldn't help myself—I gave Brad a hard kick in the ribs after I had it in my hands. As I kicked him, I thought, *Oh jeez. This is how it starts; I'm heading down the road to a life of ruthless violence.* I felt so bad about that, I kicked him again. Extra hard. Then I warned, "Make any noise at all, dirtbag, and I shoot."

I heard Brad stifle a chuckle, so I kicked his head. I was beginning to enjoy it. Me and Uma. We could be twins after all. Fraternal twins, anyway.

The fake cops knocked hard. "Everything all right in there? Police. Open the door. We got a call about a disturbance."

The four of us stayed quiet, and Brad must have been sick of getting kicked, because he didn't even groan. Dusty started barking in a regular rhythm and trotted over to the door.

My mother yelled out, "Everything's fine here, officer. We're all just fine. Thanks for your concern."

"We need to verify that, ma'am. Open the door now."

Dusty was still barking when I saw a shadow move past the den window and realized one of them was coming around to the sliding glass door leading into the den, where we all just happened to be. The curtains were drawn, but it wouldn't take much, I figured, for this dude to get in that door. "One of them's coming around the back." I whispered loud enough for all of us to hear.

"My gun, Annabelle, give me my gun." That's when I remembered that there were two guns, and Mickey's was still in Brad's pocket. I squatted down and pulled it out, handed it to Dad, and he gave it to Mickey. "Now, Sylvia and Jeff, get out of here. Go upstairs into the bathroom and lock the door." Mickey was whispering, too.

Mom started to protest, but Mickey ordered, "Now." He can do that. He takes control and gets everyone to do what needs to be done. He's a natural leader. A guy you'd walk through fire for. A guy who can make you believe that a spontaneous trip to Las Vegas is the best idea anyone ever had, ever.

Dad helped Mom up and after giving me a look of, I have to say, full terror, he led her upstairs, saying, "Mick, you don't let anything happen to our daughter."

Mickey rolled over on his stomach and propped himself on his forearms, holding his gun in both hands and pointing it at the sliding glass door. "Get down, Annabelle. Keep your gun on Brad, but take cover."

The recliner Brad had been sitting in was between me and the door, so I knelt down behind it and stuck the gun into Brad's side. "Don't you move," I whispered. Dusty stopped barking and started growling, still at the front door.

A cement garden urn came hurtling through the glass, pulling the curtain with it and landing a few inches from Mickey. Jake followed, gun raised, and in the next second, he was down on the floor. I heard Mickey fire, and I figured he got Jake. Dusty barreled in, barking, and slid across the wood floor, crashing into me, knocking me over on my side. I pointed the gun toward the broken door and pulled the trigger. Then we heard a loud "Shit!" and someone running.

That's when the good guys showed up.

Chapter Twenty-six

I rode in the ambulance with Mickey to the hospital again, and I waited while they stitched up his thigh—like Mom said, he was lucky, as the bullet didn't hit a major artery or the bone. We gave statements over and over again to the police, that night and the next day.

Mickey did manage to shoot one of the bad guys. He didn't die, but he won't escape jail. The other guy was running to the car when the real police showed up; they hauled his ass off in the squad car.

My bullet, on the other hand, ended up lodged in the den wall just above the door. Talk about recoil.

As for Jake, well, he did die. But not because Mickey shot him. Jake lost his balance throwing that urn at us. He was falling to the floor before Mickey fired, and the bullet missed him. The urn busted in two, and he landed on a sharp edge of a broken side. That is, his neck did. Got his carotid artery *that* time. He was dead pretty fast. I won't lie to you: it was a big sickening bloody mess.

Brad Slimebag Franklin got away with nothing. The police searched his car and found a tire iron with Cassie's blood on it. He had used it to pry open the door and hit her with it, too. He confessed so he wouldn't get the needle at San Quentin, but he'll spend the rest of his life there.

Mary was arrested at SFO just as she was about to board a plane for Rio. Georgia was apprehended outside of Great Falls,

Montana, a few days later. She had fled as soon as Mickey and I had left her office. I guess she was going to head north into Canada, as far away from Mary and Jake as possible.

Both women spilled their guts to the police, filling in all the details.

Georgia hatched the whole plan. She and Jake had teamed up at the casino in Vegas to embezzle some money, but Georgia chickened out on the deal at the last minute. When she quit the casino and moved to San Francisco, she decided to cash in on old people by specializing in estate law.

Jake had been pissed about her splitting and had been threatening her ever since. So Georgia invited Jake to join her in the Tall Oaks scheme, to get him off her back and out of her life. Together they decided to bring Mary in, since she was such an accomplished thief, and Georgia finagled that room for her.

Mary's role was to suss out the likely victims—plus steal their jewelry. Georgia would gain their trust—and their checks made out to her phony investment company. Withdrawals required two signatures, Jake's and Mary's. Once a month all three would go get the cash and secure it in the strong box within the safe deposit box. The three keys—Mary's and Georgia's strongbox keys hidden in the hatpins and Jake's safe-deposit-box key—were insurance. Not one of them could make off with the dough without the others.

Once Mary was out of rehab she had to tell Jake about the missing hatpins, and that's when Jake got Brad—his old police academy buddy—involved.

When Brad couldn't find the hatpins at my apartment, he called Jake, who gave him Georgia's number and told him to warn her that if she really did still have the key, then she was in trouble not only with Jake, but with Brad, who could arrest her.

Brad was right about Mary being afraid of her own son. She had texted him Luis' medallion number when she saw us running out of the Royal Opal. That's how Jake found us at The Full House, but by then she figured I didn't have the hatpin on me and didn't want to run into him any more than we did.

She called him after she left the Sleep Tight Inn and told him I didn't have the glasses case, and that she was going back to Tall Oaks. He hired his cronies—those two fake cops with the wrong shoes—to bring her to him. He didn't trust her and was royally pissed about the missing hatpins.

Mickey went back to New York. As he put it, he had to "check in with his life." I didn't like that phrase. It seemed to imply that the past few days had been something other than his life, that *I* was something other than his life. I drove him to the airport in the Mustang. We checked his suitcase at the curb and hugged each other hard before he walked on crutches into the terminal. I waited for him to turn around and wave, but he didn't. I knew he was in pain, so I tried not to read anything into that. Maybe he wasn't good at goodbyes. And he said that it wasn't really "goodbye." He said he'd call me in a couple of days. I turned in the rental car and got a cab back to Mom and Dad's.

I asked Mom about the clock. She told me that after she found me looking at it that morning when Mickey and I spent the night, she was inspired to take it into a repair shop, realizing that she never would fix it herself. "I didn't tell Jake about it because he'd just kill us right away, rather than tear the house apart looking for it, that fucker."

The police called the repairman to ask him he had found anything unusual in the clock. He said as a matter of fact, there was a pretty little hatpin taped to its back, inside. Now the clock is on her bookshelves, chiming each hour.

The police found more than ten million in cash and jewels in the strongbox. It's all going back to the people who were robbed at Tall Oaks.

That was the good news out of all of this mess—along with the fact that Nana truly hadn't been murdered. We confirmed that a nurse was at her bedside when she stopped breathing.

I called Cassie's mother, Beth. She was back in Philadelphia. She said she doesn't blame me for Cassie's murder, but the truth is, Cassie would be alive if she hadn't been staying at my apartment.

I also met Kirsten, Cassie's lover. We had a glass of wine at Maxfield's Bar at the Sheraton Palace. I liked her all right, but we were uneasy around each other. I got the sense that she wanted to forget about Cassie more than she wanted to remember her. We didn't have a second glass.

The two days after Mickey left turned into four, then six. I left a couple of messages for him, but he didn't call me back.

I took a leave of absence from work. I couldn't concentrate. I couldn't face living in my apartment, so Bonkers and I moved in with Mom and Dad for a while. Dusty wasn't too happy about Bonks.

Dad sat up late with me most nights and we watched old movies. Lots of them had happy endings—riding-off-into-the-sunset kind of stuff. The heroes always turned around and waved goodbye. They made me cry, cuddled in the cradle of Dad's shoulder.

I'd go from pining for Mickey to being furious with him. A lot of this stuff was my fault, if you can call it that, fault. But it wasn't like I knowingly led him into anything, and it was his lousy idea to go to Las Vegas in the first place. Each day without hearing from him made me sad, then mad, then I'd forgive him, and then I'd watch another movie.

Then he called.

He asked me to meet him at a café not far from Union Square at two the next day. "We have some unfinished business, and I don't want to do it over the phone."

This made me nervous. He didn't say that he loved me, or that he missed me. Was he the next guy in my life to move on? I was sick of playing Joan Cusack. I wanted to be Ione Skye in *Say Anything,* when John Cusack is so in love with her that he stands in her driveway at night and holds his boom box over-head playing Peter Gabriel's "In Your Eyes." Okay, so they were teenagers, just out of high school. It was still a great moment.

But if Mickey was going to dump me, he was right about one thing. He'd have to do it in person. I told him I'd be there, and hung up the phone.

Chapter Twenty-seven

I was sitting at a sidewalk table outside the café, my left leg bouncing up and down while I played with an empty sugar packet, its contents already dumped into my cappuccino. Mickey came up behind me and touched my shoulder. I jumped about a mile in the air and knocked my coffee all over the table. Scared the crap out of me. "Jeez! Mickey!"

He was still wearing an eye patch, and he was using a cane—for his leg, not his sight. Nice cane, too, with a brass eagle handle. Mickey. Always stylish.

He leaned on it and smiled at me. "Hi."

"Hi."

He bent toward me and gave me a little hug, then limped over to the other chair and sat down.

"How's the leg?"

"Good. Sore, but getting there." He pulled out the chair and sat down. "How are you?"

"Good. Sore, but getting there." I gave him a weak smile. I took a paper napkin and started mopping up the spilled coffee, not very well.

The waitress came and took Mickey's order for a double espresso, then went back inside. Mickey looked at me. "Why are you sore?"

This was a little hard to take. "Um, well, I haven't heard a peep from you for ten days, and now you show up all of a sudden, and

I don't know what's going on with you, and if you're going to end it all right here, then just do it and get it over with. I mean it. I have things I have to do." Actually, I had nothing to do.

But Mickey didn't say anything until the waitress brought his espresso, set it down after wiping up the table with a rag, and left. He took a sip. "Good coffee." He took another sip. Then he just sat there. It made me nervous. I picked up my dripping cup and took a sip of nothing—it had all been spilled.

"Walbon," he finally said.

"Walbon?"

"The computer tech guy."

My heart rate doubled in a nanosecond. "What...?"

"I looked up the case. Carol Simpson, your customer service manager, didn't end up pressing charges, but there was still a record of the beating. I found him. Jerry Walbon."

"Where?"

"Seattle. Moved there about six months ago."

"And? Jeez, Mickey, just tell me what you've done!"

He laughed. "Like what, bust his kneecaps or leave a horse head in his bed? I didn't do anything, Annabelle. Didn't have to. Rapists usually keep raping. His last victim got him busted. He was convicted about a month ago, and now he's in jail."

I tilted my head straight back to face the sky and sucked in a deep lungful of air. "Thank you for finding this out."

"You're welcome." Mickey took another sip.

After my heart rate slowed to normal range, I sat up straight.

"So, loose ends all tied up, everything's over, and we can get on with our lives."

"Something like that. But not quite."

"Meaning...?"

Mickey reached across the table and held out his hands, wiggling his fingers in invitation. I edged in and tentatively placed my hands in his, not sure if I should.

His come-hither deep brown eye searched every inch of my face before he broke a smile. "I'm sorry about the last ten days. Actually, I'm sorry about the last ten days, seven hours, and..."

he looked at his watch "…thirty-two minutes. I had to check in with my precinct, follow up with the extortion case, see my doctor about my leg, an eye doc about my eye; I had to pay bills, check in with my grandmother, call a few friends, and…"

I interrupted. "But not me. You couldn't even *return* my calls?" I tried to pull my hands away, but Mickey held them tightly.

"No. I know that was rude, but I had to be sure."

"That I'm not a crazy criminal?"

"Will you stop interrupting me, Annabelle? Will you please stop? I'm trying to tell you something serious, here."

I closed my eyes and waited. *Now he will tell me that it's just not going to work, just like in* The Notebook, *when Ryan Gosling and Rachel McAdams break up.* "Okay, go ahead." I kept my eyes closed.

"I had to be sure that I cannot in any real sense get on with my life without you. I had to try it, to make sure. And I only made it for ten days, seven hours, and…thirty-four minutes."

That got me. I opened my eyes, which immediately filled with tears. "I'm a wreck," I choked.

Mickey nodded. "I know."

"But you love me?"

"I do."

"I love you, Mickey. God I do. I haven't felt safe without you. I haven't felt anything but sad and scared and confused."

"Can you trust me? Like you said, I was a big fat liar. And I've stayed away from you for ten days."

"And seven hours and thirty-six minutes."

"Are you sure you can let me back into your heart?"

I took a deep breath and wiped the back of my hand across my nose. Mickey handed me a napkin, but it was wet with coffee, so he dropped it on the table. I hoped my hand would air dry. I sniffed a few times until I regained a modicum of control. I found my voice. "You never left my heart. It's a little bit broken, but now I have good reason to kick your ass anytime I want to." I made myself smile.

Mickey slapped the table, clattering the cups, and laughed. "Aaah. I get it. I'll be paying for this the rest of my life."

"I hope so."

"Me, too." He took my hands again, even though one of them was snotty. "My ophthalmologist said that UC Med would be a great choice for my eye surgery. I'm having it done tomorrow. Will you go with me?"

"Yes."

"Are you back in your apartment?"

"No. I've been staying at my parents'."

"How are they?"

"Good, all things considered. The door and furniture are fixed. I think they're still stunned by their daughter taking on a gang of criminals. They'll be happy to see you."

"Do you like New York City?"

My heart soared. My face must have lit up like a full moon with cauliflower ears turning bright red, peeking out from under my white felt fedora. "I *love* New York City." I hurried around the table to sit on Mickey's lap, until I caught a look of alarm in his eyes and remembered his leg. I hesitated, but he guided me down to rest on his left leg while he moved the right out of the way. I slid my arms around his neck. "But only if Bonkers can come."

Mickey kissed me. His lips felt just as soft and good as they did that first kiss in Las Vegas. "Doesn't he love it at your parents'? Wouldn't he be happier there?" I shook my head slowly, my eyes beaming dire threats. "Oh, all right. Do you think he'll stop biting me?" He kissed me again.

"You'll learn how to play with him. We'll get lots of Band Aids." I kissed him back. We couldn't stop kissing.

"I want to take you to Maine, to meet my grandmother."

"I want to do that more than anything in the world. Well, almost," I murmured, and kissed him again. A couple of teenagers walked by and giggled. We were something of a spectacle for passersby. I pulled away from him, stood up, and dragged my chair around next to his and sat down.

Mickey gently took my hand. "There's something else."

My heart jumped again. "What?"

"Luis."

"Luis! You've talked to him? I haven't talked to him since, well, you know…"

"Yes. In fact, he flew to New York and spent a couple of days with me. We're starting a business."

"Mickey, are you NUTS? You don't want to drive cabs in…"

Mickey grinned and waved me off. "Not driving cabs, you maniac. We're going to start a PI firm. Ruby, Luis' wife, has had enough of Las Vegas, and Luis figures he has, too. Time for a change. It's something I've wanted to do for a while—strike out on my own."

It took me a minute to comprehend PI. "Private investigation? Wow."

"Wow is right. Wanna job?"

"Gee, Mickey, I don't know, I don't think I like guns, and I…"

"…solved a murder, remember? Anyway, no need for you to shoot any guns. You can run the office. Answer phones. Do some research. And dumpster diving."

"DUMPSTER DIVING? Now that's hard to refuse. Good pay?"

Mickey laughed again. "Good pay."

"Am I a partner?"

He pulled back from me a bit, his eyes glistening. "But of course! The name of the business will be "Paxton, Maldonado & Starkey: Private Investigations."

I stood up. "That's too long!" I paced on the sidewalk while Mickey watched me. I was thinking out loud. "We could call it PMS, Private Investigations…Yikes, no, that's terrible. Can't do that." I kept thinking. "It should be something witty, not with our names.…" I stopped pacing. "I've got it."

Mickey pulled out his wallet and left money on the table for the coffees. "I'm listening."

"Hatpin Investigations."

"No."

"C'mon, Mickey, it's fun, it's great, it's…"

"It's stupid, Annabelle, I'm sorry, but it's stupid."

He was right. It was stupid. But we were going to be partners, and I didn't want him to have the upper hand from the get go. So I laughed. "You might be right, but I'm not giving up on it yet."

Mickey stood up. "The name can wait. But I can't wait any longer to see you naked."

"Hmm…is that so?"

"Mm hmm." He took my hand and we walked further up the street. "My hotel is right up here, and I have a very nice suite."

"I don't like the sound of that, if you want to know the truth. The last time we went to a very nice suite…"

Mickey pulled me to him, hugging me. He whispered, "This one is already stocked with two bottles of pinot noir, and I've ordered two big plates of steaming hot French fries and two big bowls of vanilla ice cream with chocolate sauce ready to be delivered immediately upon my phone call to the floor's butler."

Being held so tightly and hearing that voice in my ear made me breathless again. I giggled. "What's the name of this place with the butler on every floor?"

"Hotel Paris. It's brand new. Someday I'll take you to the real place."

We walked slowly to the hotel, with Mickey needing help from his cane and looking like an exotic multinational pirate who had met up with the wrong end of a sword. I looped my left arm through his right and stuck my right hand in my pants pocket, fingering the mountain lion fetish I now carry with me all the time.

I had a flash of memory…the end of a great old movie I watched recently, but which one? I let it go. This was my great ending, and mine alone.

To receive a free catalog of Poisoned Pen Press titles, please contact us in one of the following ways:

Phone: 1-800-421-3976
Facsimile: 1-480-949-1707
Email: info@poisonedpenpress.com
Website: www.poisonedpenpress.com

Poisoned Pen Press
6962 E. First Ave. Ste 103
Scottsdale, AZ 85251